NO POWER
A BRONXLAND NOVEL

TODD KIRBY

For The Bronxhearted.

———

Ne Cede Malis.

PROLOGUE

The skyline of the Upper East Side twinkles in the distance, but the rough, black waters of the Harlem River reflect none of it. Waves slosh and churn like oil in a hot tub, and when a gang of dark clouds smother the full moon, it begins.

Halfway across the river, a subtle red glow appears beneath the waves and intensifies as it rises to the surface, like a sunken stop light being reeled in by an unseen fisherman. The radiant water glows a dazzling electric red, and begins steaming and swirling violently, when suddenly —

A large droplet of fiery lava breaches the surface. As the ring of lava spreads outwards, something starts bubbling up in its darkened center until finally, that *thing* breaches the surface.

It's nearly impossible to make out in the choppy waters, but when it exhales air through a powerful blowhole, a red glowing mist explodes upward, partially illuminating the arched, hairy spine of a black, barnacled creature.

As quickly as it arose, the creature dives back down below the surface, leaving behind a black pool in the center of the blazing lava that looks like a pupil surrounded by a devilish, blood-red iris. The lava descends back into the depths of the Harlem River, and the waters fall dark.

But the faint flicker of an electric red substance remains.

1

RICH KID

Tom Walton stood with his forehead pressed against the glass of his floor to ceiling windows on East 72nd Street, peering out at the New York City skyline. His eyes looked especially hollow for a young man contemplating how to spend his seventeenth birthday.

A knock at the door snapped him from his trance.

"What, Rosa?"

Wearing an open golden bathrobe with a matching pair of European briefs underneath, Tom made no effort to conceal his pale, nearly-nude body as he turned to see a sturdy Hispanic woman stepping into the room. Rosa, his live-in housekeeper, smiled from ear to ear, holding a muffin with a birthday candle in it.

"Feliz Cumpleaños, Mr. Walton."

Unmoved by the gesture, Tom replied, "G'mornin'."

"No es morning. It's six p.m.."

The sun was going down, not up, Tom realized. It was bound to happen when breakfast consisted of polishing off a bottle of Casamigos at Artichoke Pizza after a night of clubbing.

He turned to Rosa and nodded at the candle.

"You can blow it out," he said.

Rosa looked disappointed.

"You don't want to make a wish?" she asked.

Tom scoffed, "Wishes are for poor people."

Tom walked to his private bathroom and started pissing with the door open, actively splashing the toilet seat that he didn't bother putting up.

Rosa shook her head. She held the muffin in front of her face, closed her eyes to search for a wish, then blew out the candle.

"Your father called," she told Tom. "He's in the city tonight and made a dinner reservation for you two."

Tom rolled his eyes, then flushed the toilet and tied his robe closed.

"What restaurant?" He asked.

"Bond Street Grill."

Tom sneered, *such plebeian tastes.*

Rosa opened a gigantic closet door and began putting together an outfit for Tom. Her voice muffled by the thick jungle of clothes, she called out, "He also asked me to find out what you wanted for your birthday."

How about a father who knows, Tom thought. But he didn't say it. He knew that showing emotion was a sign of weakness. Besides, *he* didn't even know what he wanted for his birthday; he was already sitting on a twenty million dollar inheritance, had vacationed in every civilized country in the world, and had hooked up with a bottle service girl from every night club in the Meatpacking District — except for one.

Tom turned to his bed, "Hey!"

Something stirred underneath the white silk sheets, and a beautiful blonde woman in her early twenties slowly emerged. She sat up in bed, wearing only a bra, paying no mind to Rosa.

"Ya?" She asked, in what sounded like an Eastern European accent. It reminded Tom of the dentist's office: *open wide and say "ah."*

"What club do you work at again?" He asked.

"Excess," she responded with pride.

A hollow feeling grew in Tom's stomach. It was not the reaction he expected to have, since crossing Excess off his list meant he'd successfully conquered them all. But the accomplishment evoked no sense of gratification; just the sad realization that he officially had nothing to look forward to.

"Cool," Tom said, visibly numb. "Feel free to leave soon."

Offended, the woman turned to Rosa in disbelief, but Rosa kept her gaze on Tom. Tom paid her bills, after all.

"Mr. Walton," Rosa inquired gently, "Any ideas for your birthday gift?"

It was unclear if Tom heard the question, as he mindlessly grabbed his cell phone and began thumbing around. Seconds later, the sounds of passionate moaning emanated from the device, filling the room, and Tom's hollow eyes became glued to a raunchy porn video playing on screen. Tom was checked out, stuck in a depressive trance that Rosa was beginning to see more and more frequently.

"What is something that makes you feel good, Mr Walton?" Rosa asked, determined to figure out this gift.

"Forget feeling good," Tom said. "It's about not feeling bad. And Maddy Longlegs seems to be distracting me pretty well right now."

Tom tossed his phone over to Rosa, the sounds of adult film star Maddy Longlegs' pleasurable moans still filling the room. Rosa checked the video, and was immediately repelled by the images. Disappointed, Rosa sauntered out of the room with Tom's phone in hand.

Tom turned around to find the blonde woman slowly getting dressed. It was taking so long, it made Tom anxious.

"Can you get out now?" Tom said, motioning to his nightstand. "There's money in the top drawer for you."

She glared at him, enraged, "I'm not a prostitute, you spoiled little prick!"

Unfazed, Tom returned to his window and leaned his forehead against the glass. Tom felt misunderstood, but he didn't care enough to defend himself. The truth was, Tom knew the woman wasn't a prostitute, and he had never paid for a woman's company; he just knew it was the quickest way to get a woman to leave.

Behind him, the woman stormed towards the door and when she passed the nightstand, she paused. Inside the open drawer was a seemingly bottomless pile of cash, collected in stacks of hundred dollar bills. The woman reached down, snatched multiple stacks, and rushed out.

Tom didn't bother checking to see how much money was left in his drawer, because it didn't matter; he didn't plan on living long enough to spend it all anyway.

SENATOR WALTON WAS NEVER on time for family. But since he had somewhere else to be, he was sitting at the table alone at five minutes past eight, eyeing his Rolex and fuming that his son had the nerve to show up late.

Finally, an expressionless host arrived at the table, leading Tom to his seat. The host pulled out Tom's chair, and Tom took a seat.

"Dad."

Chester Walton, Democratic Senator of New York, ignored the greeting and frowned as he assessed his son's appearance.

"Take it easy on the booze, son. You look like dog shit."

Tom thought he looked alright. Rosa had good taste; she dressed him in a six thousand dollar outfit that he picked up during fashion week in Miami. Tom figured his dad must be picking up on the black bags under his eyes, which seemed like they were becoming permanent.

"Yeah, I haven't been feeling too good lately," Tom confessed.

"Binge drinking will do that," his father replied, unmoved.

Tom used to feel uncomfortable breaching these sorts of topics with his father, but he was so numb — and painfully hungover — that his filter was gone.

"It's more than the drinking," Tom blurted out.

Senator Walton furrowed his brow.

"What, Rosa not feeding you properly? If that's the case, tell me. There's a thousand other illegals just like her that are ready to take her place."

Tom shook his head, "No, Rosa's fine."

"Then I don't understand."

Of course you don't, Tom thought, *and that's part of it.*

Senator Walton was waiting for his son to elaborate, but Tom knew it wouldn't go anywhere. He'd end up hearing some crap about how ungrateful he was and how he had nothing to complain about. That's how it went the last time he brought up feeling depressed.

So Tom brushed the topic aside with a wave of his hand.

"Forget it," Tom said.

"Forgotten. I ordered you the lobster."

Senator Walton poured a glass of wine for each of them, then held up his glass for a toast.

"To your birthday," he said, flashing Tom a mechanical smile.

They clinked glasses, then sipped in silence. Tom always wondered why dinner with his father felt less like a family get together and more like an employee meeting with their boss. Not that Tom knew what having a job felt like; the only thing he'd ever worked on outside of school was learning how to photoshop the acne off his face for his Bumble profile. The app didn't know he was underage, and neither did the women, but he knew that the blemishes and flare-ups might raise some red flags.

"Hear back from any universities yet?" Asked Senator Walton.

"Yeah, got a few more early acceptance letters. Princeton, Yale, Stanford —"

"And Harvard?"

Tom hesitated for a beat, before responding, "Not yet."

"*Hm.*"

Tom hated that sound. *Hm.* It was one of many ways his father could make him feel worthless without even saying a word.

"How's the basketball?" Senator Walton asked, trying to revive the conversation he'd just murdered.

"It's good," Tom replied. "Became the second all-time leading scorer in Manhattan Prep history last week."

"Wow," the Senator said, halfheartedly. "That's something."

"Yeah, it was cool. They stopped the game and made a whole big thing about it."

Senator Walton raised his eyebrows ever so slightly, clearly not impressed. He took a sip of wine, then set his glass back down and looked at his son.

"You know who holds the record for the most silver medals in Olympic history?"

Tom contemplated the random trivia, then shook his head.

"I have no idea."

Senator Walton leaned back in his chair and smirked.

"Exactly."

Senator Walton stared at Tom until his point sank in. When it finally did, Tom looked deflated. The table fell silent, and it remained that way as a waiter in a white tuxedo dropped off a pair of lobsters then cleared the area.

"Why are you here?" Tom asked his father.

Senator Walton looked taken aback by the question, "For your birthday."

"Since when do birthdays matter to you?"

Before the Senator could respond, a suited man wearing an earpiece sheepishly approached the table, "Senator, our guests have arrived. They're upstairs waiting for the meeting to begin."

"Thanks Rick," Senator Walton said. "Give me two minutes."

The sheep bowed and hurried off. Senator Walton turned to his son, who was wearing a look of "*I told you so.*"

"Well, this was fun," The Senator said. "Come on, I'll walk you out."

Tom exited the restaurant to find a Bentley limousine idling curbside. His father came up behind him.

"Looks like your ride's here."

Tom turned to his dad, confused.

"What's this?"

"Open it up," the Senator said, a mischievous smirk on his face.

Tom opened the door and peered into the back seat, where Maddy Longlegs, the adult film star that he'd been admiring earlier, was sipping on a cocktail with her legs crossed, miniskirt pulled high. Tom was stunned; he couldn't believe that Rosa had actually relayed the information to his father, nor could he believe that his father had complied.

"Hi Tom," she said, in a sultry voice that made Tom blush.

Tom waved to her, then closed the car door and turned to his father. The Senator wore a proud look on his face.

"Happy Birthday, son."

Tom nodded with appreciation, wondering if the moment might even warrant a hug. Instead, Senator Walton smacked Tom's left shoulder like a distant teammate.

"Have fun," he said. "She wasn't cheap."

Suddenly, a loud commotion stole their attention. They turned to see a young Black man fighting his way through the Senator's security team. The man rushed towards Tom and the Senator, but the recording device in his hand indicated he was just a relentless reporter.

"Senator Walton!" The reporter screamed. "Dom Willis from *The New York Chronicle*. What do you have to say to people in the underprivileged communities whose hospitals you're closing?"

As Dom Willis from *The New York Chronicle* got up close to Senator Walton, the Senator turned away, looking disgusted.

The reporter heaved another question, "Are you aware that by converting outer borough hospitals into condos, you're creating a healthcare desert where the impoverished are left to fend for themselves?"

The reporter held the recorder up to the Senator's face, but the Senator slapped it aside, sending the device flying to the curb. Finally, the security team grabbed the reporter.

"You people have no class," Senator Walton blurted out.

The reporter's eyes went wide.

"You people? What the—?!"

The reporter fought desperately to break free from the security team, but he was overpowered. As they carried him away across the street, Senator Walton called out:

"My message to the underprivileged hasn't changed in thirty years. We live in a meritocracy. If poor people got off their lazy asses and worked harder, maybe they wouldn't have to scrape by, living as a bottom feeder like you!"

The reporter became even more enraged. Tom looked frightened by the seething man's eyes, but he turned to find his father looking cool, calm, and collected. In fact, he appeared to be smiling.

Senator Walton chuckled and shook his head.

"Fucking animals," he mumbled.

Tom soaked in the moment, then bent down and picked up Dom Willis's recording device that was dropped in the tussle. Senator Walton motioned to the device —

"Toss that for me, will you? I've got the developers inside waiting."

Tom nodded and shoved the recorder into the front pocket of his Balenciaga jeans.

"Is that true?" Tom asked. "You're turning hospitals into condos?"

"We sure are. But don't worry, I'll make sure you get dibs on the top floors." Senator Walton winked to his son, "Enjoy yourself tonight."

The Senator hurried back into the restaurant, and Tom watched him go. Finally, Tom turned and popped the door to the Bentley, then paused to take one last look at the reporter, who was still throwing a fit with the Senator's security team across the street. The man's display of fury intrigued Tom. He wondered, for a moment, what it might feel like to have something worth fighting for. But deep down inside he knew he never would.

"Cell phones in the box," said the slender woman working the door.

Tom and Maddy Longlegs were standing at the entrance of a penthouse apartment, where a party was raging inside. The slender woman was collecting cell phones in a golden lock box.

Tom turned to Maddy, who looked confused.

"They collect cell phones so there are no leaks," he explained. "Standard practice ever since that video of Mayor Bancroft's daughter got out. Whole world saw her twerking wearing nothing but a Jason mask."

Maddy nodded, and they both handed over their cell phones and stepped inside the party.

Tom and Maddy didn't say much to each other during the car ride over. Tom was busy fielding calls from his high school friends asking him what sort of drugs he wanted them to bring to the party. The answer was obviously *all of them*.

"So whose party is this?" Maddy asked.

"This is my buddy Westley's place. Been my best friend since I was six —-"

"DAMN RIGHT, SON!"

An animated, goofy White kid, who'd been mistaken for

Machine Gun Kelly on more than one occasion, threw his arm around Tom and smiled at Maddy.

"I'm Westley," he said.

"Maddy."

"I know who you are," said Westley, a devious look on his face.

Westley turned to Tom.

"You gotta tell me how she is."

Westley's vibe was creepy, even by Tom's standards, so Tom quickly changed the subject.

"Thanks for doing this, man. I appreciate it."

Westley looked confused.

"Doing what?"

"Throwing this party…"

Westley still didn't get it, so Tom reminded him, "For my birthday."

Westley couldn't tell if Tom was serious. After a beat, Westley burst out laughing.

"Oh, I didn't throw this for you, dog. I was already having a party, and the dates just kinda matched up. But that's cute that you think I'm such a thoughtful friend."

Westley nodded to Maddy.

"Come say hi when you're done with this little softie."

Westley rustled Tom's hair and walked away to rejoin the party.

"That's your *best* friend?" Maddy asked.

Tom nodded and stared blankly into the crowd. Finally, he turned to her —

"Wanna get blacked out?"

TWO SHOT GLASSES slammed down on the kitchen counter. Tom and Maddy wiped their mouths, reeling from the shots of tequila. Tom immediately reached for the bottle of booze and began refilling their glasses, as Maddy Longlegs scanned the party, taking in the surrounding debauchery. When she spotted a group of strung-out teenagers huddled around the opposite end of the marble countertop, chopping up tiny white crystals using black AMEX cards, she looked more concerned than entertained.

"How old are you again?" She asked.

Tom took another shot of tequila.

"Seventeen... at midnight."

Tom motioned for Maddy to enjoy the shot that he'd poured for her, but Maddy continued staring at Tom, seemingly blown away by the reality of Tom's lifestyle. Finally, she broke eye contact, and continued taking in the scene unfolding around her.

"Jesus," she mumbled under her breath.

"What?"

Maddy shook her head, then turned around to avoid Tom's gaze. Tom looked at her, curious.

"What were you going to say?" he asked.

With her back to Tom, Maddy continued shaking her head.

"No, seriously. I want to know."

Finally, Tom stepped away from the kitchen counter to get a look at Maddy's face. He was shocked to see tears streaming down her cheeks. Maddy tried to wipe them away, smearing her mascara in the process.

"It's just so sad," she said.

"I agree," Tom said. "Drunk crying after two shots is embarrassing."

Unable to stop the tears from flowing, Maddy was clearly overwhelmed. Feeling way out of his element, Tom did the best he could to comfort her —

"Maybe you should switch to champagne... makes me feel better when I feel sad."

Maddy looked at Tom with pity on her face. Finally, she reached into her purse, dug out a massive stack of cash and placed it on the countertop in front of Tom.

"I can't do this," Maddy said. "I'm sorry. I'll be praying for you."

Maddy turned and hurried away. Tom scoffed in disbelief.

"*You're* gonna pray for *me*? You're the pornstar!"

People turned to see Tom yelling at Maddy across the party. They whispered amongst themselves, pointing fingers and laughing.

Tom watched her disappear into the crowd, then turned back to his bottle of tequila. Suddenly, Westley swept in, threw his arm over Tom's shoulder, and tried to peer over the crowd to catch a final glimpse of Maddy.

"Damn, bro! You know your game needs work when a pornstar won't even bang you." Westley cackled like a hyena, then helped himself to Maddy's shot of tequila. As he wiped his mouth, he picked up the stack of cash and inspected it.

"Don't trip," Westley said. "She wasn't worth ten grand anyway."

Westley tossed the money over to Tom. Embarrassed, Tom stuffed the cash in his jacket pocket. Westley noticed the grim look on Tom's face.

"Come on," Westley said, "Let's go mess with the Coast Guard."

BOBBING up and down in the choppy waves of the East River, Tom and Westley sat on a pair of idling jet skis, engines humming next to a private dock. The fluorescent accent lights on the decked-out jet skis cycled through intense colors, the reflections of which made the boys' faces look even more wild and unhinged. Westley popped the cork off a bottle of Dom Perignon, then quickly moved to catch the escaping foam with his mouth. Satisfied, he passed the bubbly over to Tom, who gulped down half the bottle before passing it back.

"They're doing the Macy's fireworks on the East side this

year," Westley said, as he nodded toward the blue and red lights of a U.S. Coast Guard patrol boat on the other side of the river, "So there's hella cops staked out for tomorrow."

Westley turned back to Tom and held up the bottle of champagne.

"You dare me?" He asked, wearing a devious smile.

Tom wasn't sure what the dare was, but he truly didn't care. He shrugged with indifference, and apparently that was all that Westley needed, because he immediately worked the throttle and jolted through the black water up the East River. Tom carelessly accelerated after him, hair blown back, blazer whipping through the wind. As Tom rode through the waves, he turned to look at the dazzling lights of Manhattan zipping by. *It doesn't make sense,* he thought. *I live on an island with so much energy, so much stimulation, so much life, but somehow I still feel dead.*

WHAP! Westley's jet ski slapped down into the water just ahead of him. Trying to get Tom's attention, Westley cooled the throttle and pointed the champagne bottle towards a nearby dock. Tom looked over to see the familiar red and blue lights of a U.S. Coast Guard patrol boat. *Game on.*

Westley cranked the throttle and Tom followed. As they approached the boat, Tom could make out two officers on board. When the officers heard the approaching jet skis, they turned on the boat's flood lights, and one of them got on the loud speaker.

"STOP WHERE YOU ARE!" The officer demanded.

But Westley kept gunning it, undeterred, and when he got within thirty feet of the officers, he cocked back and hurled the champagne bottle at the police officers! The cops ducked and the bottle whizzed past them, shattering on the dock —

"Catch us if you can, piggies!" Westley whipped a one-eighty, sending water splashing onto the boat and all over the officers, then zoomed off. The Coast Guards jumped behind the wheel and within seconds, their boat was giving chase.

Tom joined Westley, and the two boys tore through the river, headed north. Westley screamed and laughed maniacally, while Tom looked mildly entertained. This was fun the first few times they did it, but now Tom knew the outcome; unless one of them was drunk enough to fall off, they'd never get caught. Their jet skis were simply too fast. Tom peered over his shoulder to see that the cops were so far behind them, they were barely even visible. Something about it felt unfair. It was too easy.

As they continued uptown, the buildings got shorter, the lights dimmer, and the smell of the water reminded them that they were far from the Virgin Islands. Up ahead, Westley cut his engine. He turned and waited for Tom to float up next to him.

"Straight outlaw shit right there," Westley said, as he leaned over and gave Tom a pound. He went on, "Check it out, all the firework barges. You wanna get into some *real* trouble?"

Tom followed Westley's gaze and saw several barges anchored on the Western shore, each displaying a huge MACY'S sign surrounded by stacks of what could only be fireworks.

Tom tried on the idea, but it didn't seem to fit. He glanced north up the river, where the surrounding city looked dark and unwelcoming.

"I think I'm gonna keep going," Tom said.

No way Westley heard that right. Westley glanced north just to check if he missed something. Nope, still a nightmare uptown.

"There's nothing up there but the Bronx, bro. You might wanna be careful as a skinny white dude on a jet ski... not to mention, a freakin' Walton."

Tom, eyes fixated on something uptown, spoke in a tone void of emotion.

"Don't come."

Westley scoffed and shook his head, "Whatever, bro. If someone robs my jet ski, you're buying me a new one."

Westley sat back down to straddle his ride.

"Have fun dying," Westley said. He turned the jet ski around, revved the engine, and catapulted back towards the comfort of midtown Manhattan.

I just might, Tom thought, as he swiveled back to the object of his fixation. Through the shadows uptown, a row of orange street lights were inviting him towards the Willis Avenue Bridge.

Tom pulled the jet ski ashore in a little beach area on the Bronx side of the bridge, a deliberate choice to ensure that if Westley ever cared to come looking for his toy, he'd never find it. Westley was a shitty friend, Tom decided. He wondered for a second if he'd ever had a true friend. Ever since his mom died, that feeling of being connected to another human being was something he only felt during the brief moments in which his tongue was in the mouth of a female stranger. But he knew the realities of short term gratification. He compared himself to those people who needed to go skydiving just to feel alive; it's cool while it lasts, but eventually you hit the ground. The main difference was that Tom didn't feel like he'd merely hit the ground; he felt like he'd broken through it and landed directly in hell.

He looked up at the rusty, hundred year-old swing bridge, and realized that if he wanted the impact of the water to knock him unconscious — because he'd decided that drowning while conscious probably sucked — he'd have to climb up to the bridge's truss and leap off one of the structural beams. So he began his ascent.

Approaching the street, Tom could already hear the thumping of reggaeton filling the air. The rhythm was unfamiliar to him, and that made it scary. He heard a basketball dribbling and saw a group of young Black dudes jawing at each other as they were leaving a nearby basketball court. He'd only been to the Bronx once in his life, to play in a basketball day camp up at Lehman College. The kids in camp were mostly locals, and he could vividly remember how hard they played. He'd never been fouled like that in his life. But it definitely upped his game.

He reached the walkway and scurried up the side of the bridge, keeping his head down so that the passing cars didn't see his white skin and expensive outfit. Tom was about to end his life, but he was still afraid of getting mugged. It didn't make sense on a rational level, but then again, nothing did.

Up ahead, he saw an elderly woman with caramel skin chipping away at a large block of ice making flavored ice cones. *Look at that,* he thought, *just like the piragua character from "In the Heights."* He passed by the woman and smiled, feeling like he knew her in some way because he'd seen her type portrayed on stage. But when she didn't smile back, Tom felt ashamed and exposed. It was like the woman could sense by simple proximity what a piece of shit he was. Tom put his head down and walked faster.

Reaching the center of the bridge, Tom began to climb. It reminded him of his childhood days of climbing the monkey bars at Gramercy Park, but there were no foreign-born nannies to break his fall now. As Tom climbed higher, he could feel his palms starting to sweat. It got so bad that he needed to wipe his hands on his blazer every time he reached for a higher beam. Finally, Tom reached for the top beam and pulled himself up. He carefully climbed to his feet and stood upright.

The view was majestic. This was an angle of the Manhattan skyline that Tom had never seen, not even in photographs. Probably because the photographers never made it back home, Tom thought. But Tom wasn't here to sightsee. He looked down at his scuffed Dior kicks, and his brain racked focus to what awaited him down below; the Harlem River was churning and swirling in whirlpools, the occasional white foam of a breaking wave offering the only contrast to the jet black waters.

This was it. Tom took a deep breath and started inching forward on the narrow beam when he realized he hadn't really thought about what thoughts he'd like to end on. Tom was a staunch atheist, so he knew it didn't make any difference, but something about it felt incomplete. He thought it would be like tossing out a slice of pizza with just one bite to go before the crust.

It's been a lonely ride, Tom thought. It was a thought he didn't plan on having. It just came up. And then another —

I am so fucking lonely.

Tears welled up in Tom's eyes, and he laughed as they spilled over.

God! You're such a weak, worthless, loser.

As the buried emotions started shooting up like a geyser from within, Tom was losing control of himself. Screw the internal eulogy. He couldn't take it anymore. He needed to get out. He inched closer to the edge and looked down.

Fuck it.

Tom spread his arms and leaned forward. Just as his body tilted beyond the point of no return, he caught a glimpse of something strange happening in the water below —

Tom quickly reached back to try and grab the beam, but his feet went slipping out from under him. He managed to grab hold of the rusted structure, and his sweaty hands struggled for a better grip while his feet dangled below. He glanced down and saw an electric red substance glowing on the surface of the water. It was pulsating like a beating heart. Tom looked terrified, because he suddenly wanted to live; at least long enough to find out what the hell that was. Sweat dripping from his brow, Tom tried to kick and squirm to pull himself back onto the beam, when suddenly, his hands slipped —

Tom fell through the air, watching the bridge and the night sky shrink away from him, until *SMACK*! He crashed violently into the water, plunging directly into the glowing red substance, and the world went black.

2

BRONX MEMORIAL

"Did you *really* fuck that up?"

The critic in his head jolted him awake. Tom opened his eyes and winced, due in part to the blaring fluorescent lights above him, but it was primarily the pounding headache that caught him off guard.

"You didn't really want to die," said a booming voice.

Laying on his back, Tom turned to find a large Black man in light blue scrubs rolling a blood pressure machine towards his bed. Disoriented, Tom looked around, trying to get his bearings.

"I'm sorry, what?"

"If you did, you woulda jumped off the G.W. Bridge. Ain't nobody dying jumping into water from a hundred feet."

The truck-sized nurse smiled at Tom, but Tom was too foggy to respond.

"But your call for help has been answered, my brother."

The nurse took Tom's blood pressure. Tom sat up in his hospital bed and scanned the room. He noticed the floor-to-ceiling curtains were worn and tattered with cigarette holes. There were dark brown stains all over the floor.

"What a shithole," Tom said.

"That's rude as hell, but you're right. I told my wife that if I ever get shot, she better take my ass straight to the vet's office. At least they use cleaning supplies over there."

The man burst out in jovial laughter.

"I'm just playing. They don't use cleaning supplies neither."

The man cackled some more. Tom looked worried.

Tom heard someone shouting in the hallway. He couldn't see the source, but it sounded like a woman, and the warbling voice and accent indicated she was older, and from some island some-where. The shouts got louder.

"THE TIME HAS COME! THE HOUNDS HAVE RISEN!"

Disturbed, Tom looked to the nurse, his fearful eyes pleading for the brawny man to assess the situation.

Unflustered, the nurse stood up and pulled the curtain aside, "Roselle, what the hell are you doing down here? Get your ass back upstairs or I'm calling security."

Tom tried peering over the nurse's shoulder when suddenly, a woman's head burst through the curtain to the side of him! Tom reeled, and the nurse immediately restrained the intruder. Roselle, an older Haitian woman with captivating light grey irises, looked directly at Tom —

"And the scent is on *him!!!*"

Finally, a white, rail-thin security guard in an ill-fitting uniform arrived to help the nurse restrain Roselle.

"Get her back upstairs please. Roselle, if you don't chill out, they're gonna shoot you up with some more booty juice."

Unnerved, Tom watched as the woman was escorted through what looked like an abandoned Emergency Room. There were empty chairs in the waiting room, nobody behind the reception counter. The only movement was Roselle, the security guard, and the automatic sliding doors opening and closing as they moved past.

"Come on, Ros," the security guard said. "Let's get back to your room."

The nurse closed the curtain and turned back to Tom.

"Sorry about that."

Tom's voice was quiet and shaky, "What hospital am I in?"

"Bronx Memorial," the nurse replied. "Well, technically it's the hospital *formerly* known as Bronx Memorial. We're being shut down at the end of the month, which is why I'm one of like three employees in here who actually still gives a damn."

The blood pressure machine beeped, and the man unstrapped the device from Tom's arm.

"Blood pressure is good."

"So what's the hospital called now?"

"SoBro Meadows Luxury Housing."

Tom looked nervous.

"Politicians working with greedy-ass developers turning our hospitals into money grabs. Don't give a damn about people like you and me."

Tom shamefully avoided the nurse's gaze.

"Anyway, the paramedics said they couldn't find your wallet, so I'm gonna need some information from you so we can contact your parents. What's your last name?"

Tom stared at the man blankly. He thought about what Westley said; a Walton wouldn't do so well around these parts. So Tom shrugged.

"Smacked your dome on that water pretty hard, huh? Well, fortunately for you, not all of our departments have found a new home. Due to you being a danger to yourself, you're required to stay here on a seventy-two hour hold."

"Seventy-two hours!?" Tom shouted. "Yeah right."

Tom started to get up, but as soon as the nurse stood up, Tom froze. The man was gigantic, and his face meant business; there was no way Tom was escaping that room.

"It's for your own good, brother."

Tom pleaded, "Why can't you just let me go home?"

"Because we're concerned about your well-being, and we're

committed to equipping you with the skills you need to survive out there in this crazy world."

Tom sat back down. Concerned about his well-being. *Pshh.*

"On top of that, it's the law homie. It's called a fifty-one fifty. If you're a threat to yourself or others, we gotta hold you here until the docs say you're not crazy anymore."

"I'm not crazy, I just wanted to die," Tom said.

"Only a crazy person says things like that. And until you realize that fact, we need to keep you from hurting yourself. You can relax. You're in a safe environment now —"

Boom! The building's foundation shook violently and the lights cut out.

The nurse lost his balance and grabbed the hospital bed to stabilize. After a few seconds, everything fell still. The beeping and buzzing machines all shut down, and a set of dim emergency lights slowly faded on in the corridor. Eyes wide, the nurse looked over at Tom, who appeared to be seconds away from asking for a bed pan.

"Relatively safe," the nurse shrugged. "We're still in the Bronx, after all."

"PROBABLY JUST A POWER outage from every person and their mother cranking the A.C. on a hot-ass summer night. Climate change is no joke. It ain't supposed to be a hundred degrees at nine p.m.."

The nurse stood outside the curtains holding a flashlight, leaning back inside to talk to Tom. But Tom wasn't listening; he was busy running his hands through his matted hair, curiously inspecting a sticky gelatinous substance collecting on his fingers.

"Can I take a shower?" Tom asked. "I stink."

"You'll be able to shower up in Four West once this power's back on."

"Four West?"

"Adult psych unit… but don't worry, there's some kids up there too."

A door banged open in the hall and the nurse shined the light at the security guard, who was emerging from the staircase.

"Looks like the lights went out," the guard said.

"Thanks, detective," the nurse teased. "You figure out why?"

"I look like an electrician?"

"No, but for whatever reason, they hired your skinny ass to ensure the safety of this building… and a bunch of high-risk psych patients running around in the dark don't sound like a safe thing to me."

The guard looked torn. He knew the nurse was right.

"The transformers and breakers are downstairs," the nurse said. "Check it out and I'll meet you down there after I get this kid settled in."

The guard didn't like the idea. Stressed, he reached into his pocket and pulled out a cigarette. The nurse looked at him like he was nuts.

"This is a hospital, hombre. You know you can't smoke in here."

The guard put the cigarette to his mouth, fired it up, and pulled the smoke deep into his lungs. Finally, he exhaled and placed a single cig into the nurse's scrub pocket.

"When you see how many rats are down there," the guard said, "You're gonna want one too."

The guard snatched the flashlight from the nurse, crossed the emergency room and begrudgingly disappeared into the staircase.

The nurse turned to Tom.

"You ready to meet your new roommates?"

THE GUARD STOMPED his way down the stairs, scanning his cell phone for the perfect song for his rodent-warrior mission. He skipped over the first few beats of Biggie's "Victory," the LOX's "Fuck You," and finally landed on Pop Smoke's "Got It On Me." Satisfied, he turned up the volume, tucked the phone's blaring speaker into his pocket, then pulled out his pistol.

The guard's favorite part of the job was that he was able to carry. The gun made him feel safe at work. Back when the hospital was bumping, they'd have gang shootouts in the waiting room every Saturday night. The truth was, he'd never fired his gun before, because the cops were always camped out outside the hospital in paddywagons, loading up gang members like kids heading off on a school trip. But these days, even the gangsters knew they were better off bringing their wounded ones else-where. That said, he was happy to have his gun on him now. Because he friggin' hated rats.

The guard reached the bottom of the staircase, and used his keys to unlock the door. He pushed it open to find a pitch black basement; there were no emergency lights on down here. Flash-light in one hand, gun in the other, the guard pushed forward through the darkness, nose scrunched from the odor of the dank and moldy air. He scanned the walls, searching for electrical wiring, and saw nothing but glistening, rusted sewage pipes.

Clank! A metallic sound shot through the basement. The guard spun, and pointed his light in the direction of the sound. Nervous, he reached into his pocket and faded-out the volume of his music so he could listen to his surroundings. The basement fell silent, with the exception of a quiet crackling. The guard resumed scanning the basement with his light, and saw small electrical sparks softly spraying from a giant metallic box. *There it is.*

He exhaled a breath he didn't remember holding, and started to put his gun away when —

Squeeeak! A rat skittered across his foot. The guard screamed and immediately kicked it off, sending the rat flying. In the same motion, he dropped his flashlight, drew his gun and fired *three shots* towards the airborne rat. He missed all three shots, and then ducked as the bullets ricocheted through the basement. The guard caught his breath, as the echoes of gunfire and bullets pinging off sewer pipes faded away. And then, out of the corner of his eye, he saw something dart through the light beam of his cast aside flashlight.

He whipped around to get a better look, and heard something akin to footsteps puttering through the dark. Whatever it was, it was big...

Way bigger than a rat.

"Yo! Somebody there?"

The guard gripped his gun tight, and carefully moved to pick up his flashlight. He used the light to search the area, saw nothing but more leaking pipes and industrial wiring. In the distance, he re-focused on the crackling metallic box.

The guard checked his surroundings, wondering if he was seeing things or not, then slowly approached the sparking device. He arrived at the transformer, saw that it had been severely damaged from what appeared to be blunt force. Perplexed, he noticed a chunk of loose concrete next to his foot. He shined the light on the floor, and followed a trail of concrete and wet bedrock towards a gaping hole in the floor. As the guard drew nearer to the hole, he was shocked by its sheer size. It was five feet wide, and when he peered over the edge, he saw water sloshing and shimmering in the light, fifteen feet below.

What the hell...?

He spotted his blurry reflection in the waters below, then crouched down to get a closer look. Lining the walls of the tunneled hole, he saw what looked like thick claw marks cut deep into the bedrock. Tracking the marks with his light, he followed them down to the bottom where, through the reflection of the now eerily calm water, he spotted something lurching over his right shoulder. The flashlight shook in his hand, but before he could turn around, he was yanked up into the air!

The flashlight dropped into the hole, and dull sparks from the busted transformer illuminated the silhouette of a grizzly-sized creature pinning the guard to the ground, as it discharged the bizarre, cicada-like shriek of some unearthly beast. The guard screamed in agony, but unlike his music, his cries did not gradually fade out —

They suddenly cut off.

3

FOUR WEST

Sweat stains from the nurse's pecs and belly soaked through his scrubs in the shape of a demonic face as he emerged from the stairwell. He held the door open for Tom, who stepped into the corridor and immediately spotted a sign on the wall that read, *"Four West: Adult Psychiatric."*

The nurse led Tom towards a set of metal double doors, then used a plastic key card that hung from a lanyard around his neck to swipe a sensor fixed to the wall. The doors unlocked and swung open.

"You've been delivered, my brother," the nurse said. "Best of luck to you."

The nurse turned and began heading back the way they came. Tom looked panicked.

"Wait," Tom said. "What am I supposed to do?"

The nurse spun around and continued backpedaling towards the stairwell.

"Get better," he said, as if the answer was obvious. He chuckled and nodded over Tom's shoulder, "Kiki's got you from here."

The nurse pushed through the door and disappeared into the stairwell.

Kiki? Who the hell is —

"You're a long way from Cape Cod, Bryce."

Tom spun around to find a short Black girl with braids tied up above her head via a bright yellow scrunchie. Kiki's blinding smile gave way to a genuine look of remorse.

"My bad, that was cheap. I know that not *all* white boys are named Bryce and have vacation homes in Cape Cod," she said, as her smile quickly returned, "Some of them are named Chad."

Kiki couldn't keep from chuckling to herself.

She continued, "Anyway, I don't have a problem with it as long as you're not one of those *'blue lives matter'* whites."

Tom didn't know what to say. He'd definitely heard that phrase thrown around in his dad's house. Kiki's smile quickly faded.

"Say *'all lives matter'* and I'll stab you right here for missing the point."

Kiki looked at Tom with a murderous rage in her eyes, until suddenly, she burst out laughing, "I'm playing with you!" She said, "Nobody here's got anything sharp enough to stab you."

Tom stared at her, dumbfounded.

"Are you a doctor?" he asked.

"Nope!" Kiki spun around and began skipping away down the corridor.

Tom glanced back at the door to the staircase, considered following the nurse back down to E.R., but something about this girl made him curious. Tom cautiously followed, and the moment he crossed the threshold, the metal doors shut behind him and the locks automatically bolted shut. The sound echoed through the corridor.

Shit.

Out of options, Tom cautiously followed Kiki down the dark hallway, as Kiki stomped a beat with her feet, sounding like captain of the step team. To the sounds of Kiki's *boom-boom-bap-boom-boom-bap,* they approached a light at the end of the hall, which opened up into a large, multi-purpose room illuminated by a pair of construction-grade halogen lights.

Kiki turned to Tom, "Welcome to today's tour of Four West," she said, in a comically spirited voice. "Our first stop is the beloved rec room." Kiki stepped forward and motioned to their surroundings using exaggerated gestures that reminded Tom of those showcase models on The Price is Right.

"We had a TV before the blackout," Kiki pointed to a power-less TV attached to the wall. "Even had Netflix… Bad timing on your part."

Tom followed Kiki into the room and saw no more than ten people scattered about. They were all dressed in the light blue scrubs of hospital patients. Kiki led Tom past a couple of Hispanic men seated around a ping-pong table playing a game of dominoes.

"On our right, you'll find Puerto Rico versus the Dominican Republic. All night, every night."

An elderly brown-skinned man with a Puerto Rican flag tatted on his neck slammed a domino on the table and began talking smack to his white-bearded, darker-skinned competitor in Spanish. When Tom walked by, they paused the trash talking to stare at the newcomer. Tom nodded. They didn't nod back.

"Up ahead, you'll see Vaughn. Being typical Vaughn."

Kiki nodded to a tall, sinewy, Black teenager doing one-handed push-ups by himself, grunting with each rep.

"Vaughn, we got a new guy," Kiki said.

Vaughn didn't even flinch. He stayed focused, sweat shining off his swollen muscles as he growled and pumped. Kiki shrugged and turned to Tom.

"He's like that," Kiki said. "Don't take it personally."

Kiki led Tom over to a puffy blue recliner, where a pair of giant wireless headphones rested on top of an iPad.

"This is big blue. Mad comfy. If you ever feel like crap and just wanna vibe out to *Swim Good* by Frank Ocean, because who doesn't, those headphones can *bang*. The iPad is from like ten years ago, but it works."

"Frank *who*?" Tom asked.

Kiki stared at him, mouth agape.

"I'm gonna pretend you didn't just ask that," she said, then spun around and continued the tour. Clueless, Tom followed her towards a small library area, where a pre-teen Black girl with glasses sat on a chair, reading a book aloud to a trio of zonked-out adults seated on the floor.

"Whatcha reading to them today, Mo?" Kiki asked.

Mo held up the book for Kiki to see.

"The Extraordinary Lives of Insects. We're just getting into breeding. Steamy stuff. You want to join?"

"I'd love to, but I'm helping my new friend here get settled."

Mo looked at Tom and seemed surprised.

"Woah, you're a *patient*? The only caucasians in this building are doctors," she said. "Anyway, I'm Mo."

Mo and Tom exchanged waves.

"Tom."

"Damn," Kiki said, "At least Bryce has some Vanilla flavoring. Tom is white *and* bland. Like plain-ass oatmeal."

"Fuck off."

Kiki looked at Mo surprised, and they both chuckled.

"*Woo!* I like the sass, Tommy Boy. Let's keep it moving,"

Kiki continued walking, and Tom reluctantly followed.

"Good luck tonight, Kiki!" Mo called out.

Kiki yelled over her shoulder, "Thank you baby!"

Mo returned to reading about insects and Tom caught up with Kiki as she walked through the dining area. An old woman sat slumped over a table. When Tom approached, she lifted her head, and Tom recognized her as the screaming woman from downstairs. Only now, her eyes looked heavy, and saliva hung from her chin.

"That's Roselle," Kiki said. "They just gave her the booty juice, so not the most flattering introduction."

"Booty juice?" Tom asked.

"If you get out of control, the doc will give you a shot in the booty to make you calm down."

They walked past, and when Roselle saw Tom, her tired eyes flickered with recognition. Unable to use words, she began moaning at the sight of Tom.

"What's wrong with her?" Tom asked.

Kiki stopped short and turned around, looking disappointed.

"Haven't you ever seen a prison film? You don't ask people that question in here."

"This isn't a prison."

"True," she smirked, then reached up and tapped the side of Tom's head with her index finger. "But that is."

She turned, crossed the dining room and walked down another hallway. Perplexed, Tom followed. He glanced back at Roselle, unsettled by her gaze. Finally, Kiki opened the door to a room and motioned for Tom to enter.

"Here's your room. Scrubs on the bed. Schedule's on the wall. Breakfast is at eight a.m. sharp, individual therapy is at eleven... you can read, right?"

Tom glanced around the low-ceilinged room and saw dirty sheets covering two single cots. One of them was empty, while the other contained the frail body of a shirtless teenaged boy with light brown skin. He was seated in the lotus position with his eyes closed.

"That's Omar," Kiki whispered, "He recently started meditating —"

"Can y'all shut the hell up please!?" Omar yelled, his eyes still closed. "I'm in here tryna get enlightened with this lovingkindness shit but y'all motherfuckers just babbling on like you chillin' at a block party!"

Kiki looked at Tom, *oops*.

Kiki motioned for them to exit the room and return to the hallway. Once Kiki quietly closed the door behind them, Tom spoke up.

"You need to show me where the head doctor's office is," he said.

Kiki turned to Tom, ticked by his tone.

"First off, I don't *need* to do shit. I don't work for this place, and I certainly don't work for you. I'm just being a kind-ass person because it makes me feel good inside."

Tom took a cautious step back, retreating from Kiki.

She went on, "I know you think you don't belong here, that you're better than this, that this place is for people who have real problems, and not —"

"But you don't understand," Tom interjected. "I *really* don't belong here."

"Ha! You probably belong here the most," Kiki replied. "At least the others had the sense to try and drown themselves in their bathtubs and not in the Harlem River."

Tom looked perplexed, *how did she know?*

"You stink, my dude. That's how I know. Point is, Julie is the best therapist on the planet. She's the reason I went from being bed-bound to giving lively, engaging tours to boring white boys during blackouts."

"Kiki, he's ready for you," a voiced called out. They turned to find Julie, a buoyant Indian woman in her thirties walking down the hall. Her pantsuit gave her a professional look, but her vibe was all love.

"Julie!" Kiki shouted. "I was just telling Tom about how dope you are."

Julie smiled at Kiki, then shined it at Tom.

"Hi Tom, I take it you're our most recent patient to be sent upstairs without paperwork?" Tom shrugged, and Julie continued, "I would apologize for the state of things here, but it's just

reality, you know. If we can manage to find peace inside a dilapi-
dated shithole like this, we can find peace anywhere."

She extended a hand to Tom.

"Isn't she the truth?" Kiki smiled at Tom.

Even her curse words sounded professional, Tom thought. He
reached out and shook Julie's hand.

"Can you get me out of here?" Tom asked.

Julie shook her head, "That's up to Doctor Ellison."

"Can you take me to him?"

"I can, but he's got an important meeting first," Julie said,
turning to Kiki. "You ready?"

Kiki nodded with excitement.

"Remember," Julie said, "Healthy detachment and trust in the
universe."

Kiki nodded and gave Julie a hug. Tom looked at them both,
skeptical. When Kiki released the hug, she turned to Tom with a
fist bump.

"Nice knowing you. Wish me luck, Tom."

"Where are you going?" he asked.

"To find out how much longer I'll be here."

Kiki began dancing down the long hallway, *boom-boom-bap-
boom-boom-bap,* until she reached a prominent door with a small
glass window that emanated light. She knocked, then peered
through the little window. Finally, a tall, fit white man with salt
and pepper hair opened the door with a grin and let Kiki inside.
Doctor Ellison watched her enter, then glanced down the hall at
Julie and Tom, before closing and locking the door.

Julie checked her watch.

"Oh goodie, you're just in time for group therapy."

Julie led Tom down the hall, with Omar following in the
distance. Tom glanced over his shoulder and noticed that Omar,
who was now sporting a scrub shirt that was four sizes too big,

seemed to be floating, barely touching the balls of his feet on the floor as he walked, his posture miraculously erect, his eyes barely open.

"Mindful walking," Julie explained to Tom, catching his curious gaze. "This practice helps keep the mind rooted in the present moment."

Suddenly, Omar opened his eyes, "Yo Julie, what do I do if all I can think about in the present moment is that I look mad ridiculous?"

Julie smiled, "You keep practicing."

Frustrated, Omar sucked his teeth, then dropped from the balls of his feet and assumed a gangster strut that was worlds away from mindful pacing.

"Practice is over for today," Omar said, as he marched past them and led the way into the rec room.

When they entered the large room, Tom spotted eight chairs positioned in a circle. He watched Omar take a seat next to Vaughn and Mo, who were sitting in the circle chatting. Roselle sat on the other side of the circle by herself, drooling and half asleep. The rest of the seats were empty.

"Evening group is voluntary, and for our higher-functioning clients," Julie told Tom. "I have no idea where you are with functioning, but I like to give everybody the opportunity to take part. It's a place where we share our thoughts and feelings in a nonjudgmental way and try to become comfortable with vulnerability."

The thought filled Tom with dread. He suddenly felt like he had to piss.

"Where's the bathroom?" Tom asked.

"You sure it can't wait a few? You're going to miss your introduction."

"I really have to go."

Julie pointed down the hallway.

"Left at the end of the hall, third door on your right. But the emergency lights are only working along this main corridor, so you're gonna need this."

Julie took off a lanyard around her neck, which contained a little flashlight and a plastic keycard ID. She passed it over to Tom.

"You might think I'm naive for giving you the key, but I consider it a first attempt at developing trust. Also, trying to go AWOL automatically gets you fourteen more days in here. So I'd strongly advise only using the flashlight."

Tom nodded and started down the hall, when Julie called out —

"And hurry back for your introduction!"

But Tom knew he wasn't coming back.

TOM HELD the little flashlight between his teeth, shining it into the urinal as he emptied his bladder. He pushed to widen his stream, anxious to finish up so he could get the hell out of there. The bathroom was dark, as if everything beyond his beam of yellow light had been covered in jet black ink, and the thick smell of bleach was already giving him a headache. Squirt squirt, shake shake, he put his baby snake away and flushed. As Tom turned around, the light from the flashlight crossed the mirror, and something caught his eye. He stepped closer to the mirror and shut the flashlight off.

What the...?

In the total absence of light, Tom noticed his clothing glowed an oxblood red, pulsating ever so slightly. Now Tom was starting to remember. His birthday. The bridge. The substance in the water. It seemed ridiculous now that he was so curious about what was clearly just some gnarly pollution that was probably normal in the Bronx. He'd heard all kinds of stories about companies dumping toxic waste into the rivers around the outer boroughs, not on TV of course, but because his father had defended several of them in court.

Tom turned the flashlight on and noticed that the glowing became more subtle; it was barely noticeable with a light source present. He stuck the flashlight in his mouth, and began trying to wipe the substance from his hands and arms, but it was stickier than tree sap. *Screw it,* Tom thought. *I'll have Rosa fix me a bubble bath when I get home.* Tom didn't know what he'd do after that; it wasn't like he was suddenly dying to live, but he sure as hell didn't want to be imprisoned in some godforsaken hospital while he figured out next steps.

Tom left the bathroom and instead of returning the way he came, he made a left towards a pair of metal double doors. He hurried down the hall, checked over his shoulder, then scanned Julie's key card. CLANK. The locks released, and Tom pushed through. He was impressed that the folks in charge of Four West had the foresight to install battery-powered locks; they prevented Bronx psychopaths from flooding the streets during power outages like this. The doors closed behind him and the lock bolted shut.

Tom barged into the stairwell and began flying down the steps. Three, sometimes four at a time. He'd passed the marker for the third floor, then the second, and as he neared the ground floor, he slowed down. Tom peaked through a small window in the stairway door to check for anybody who might try returning him to Four West. But there were no signs of life.

Perfect.

He carefully opened the door a crack, poked his head through, and was struck by the sheer silence of the Emergency Room. It was just as he'd left it, but Tom was too dazed — and faded — at the time to truly register how eerie the setting was. Tom hadn't seen many zombie movies, since his father claimed they were films for Philistines, which he assumed was a derogatory name for people from Philidelphia, but he'd seen enough of them at

Westley's house to know that this was prime zombie shit right here.

Tom's heart rate began to jump, but he didn't know exactly why. There was no such thing as zombies, and anybody who dared to stop him from going home would be hard-pressed to find a job as a dishwasher once his father heard about it. Still, Tom could feel his stomach tying up in knots.

Tom stepped into the corridor, still holding onto the stairwell door handle, when he heard a horrific sound echo through the stairwell behind him.

A moan. An anguished moan.

Tom froze. It *was* a hospital, Tom reminded himself. People got sick and died in these places. But something about that moan sounded familiar. He took a step back into the staircase to listen.

Out of the silence came another loud moan, and then —

"*Help me...*"

The deep voice was one that Tom recognized. Tom turned his flashlight on and shined it down the staircase towards the basement, which was void of emergency lights.

"Hello? Somebody down there?"

"Please help!" The man screamed.

Something came over Tom, and before he could think himself out of it, he was hustling down the stairs into the darkness. The flashlight bounced around the walls, and once Tom turned around the first flight of stairs, his light fell on something out of a nightmare.

The hefty nurse, who'd just recently escorted Tom up to Four West, was crawling up the stairs on his stomach, and when Tom shined the light on his lower half, he saw why. His left leg, beneath the knee, was gone. Tom could immediately tell that the amputation wasn't the clean work of a surgeon. The mangled limb had left a trail of blood down to the closed basement door.

Holy fuck.

Tom reflexively knelt down next to the nurse, and could see

the man was twitching. Through labored breaths, the nurse spoke.

"Get everyone out of here."

The fear in the nurse's eyes made Tom shake. Tom wanted to ask questions, but his rational brain simply couldn't be accessed.

BOOM! A ferocious bang on the basement door. Tom shined the light on a massive dent on the steel door. Only a sledge-hammer could leave a mark like that, Tom thought, but who the hell does demolition work during a blackout?

BOOM! Another dent formed right next to it, the impact even harder this time. Tom slowly stood up, and unconsciously began to backpedal when —

BOOM!... BOOM!... BOOM! His breath quickened along with the pace of the impact. Terrified, he glanced down at the nurse, who screamed:

"GET THE FUCK OUT!"

BOOM! This time, something broke through the metal. It looked more like a claw than the end of a sledgehammer, and a deafening shriek from the other side of the basement door stroked Tom's nerves like violin strings. He made eye contact with the nurse, who urged him —

"GO!"

Tom turned and bolted up the stairs, and quickly found himself on the second floor. Adrenaline pumping, his brain wasn't doing the work. If it was, he would've exited through the first floor and escaped the hospital. The banging on the doors echoed through the stairwell, getting progressively louder, more frequent, until *BANG!* The sounds of crunching metal and concrete gave way to the nurse's agonized screams. Tom knew that the only thing separating him from whatever the hell ripped the nurse's leg off was just a couple flights of stairs. Tom got to the fourth floor and burst through the door, but the front of his shirt got caught on the handle and ripped wide open. His bare chest exposed, he raced down the hallway towards the steel double doors. He scanned Julie's keycard, rushed inside, and pulled the door closed. The latches on the door locked, but Tom tested it just in case.

Tom sprinted down the hall, sneakers squeaking on the linoleum floors, and turned the corner down the main corridor. He barged into the rec room, where Julie and the others were taking part in a quiet session of group therapy. At the sound of Tom's rushing footsteps, they turned to find him pale with fear and gasping for air, his ripped shirt hanging off to his sides like the cape of some deranged superhero.

Hysterical, Tom screamed, "We need to escape! There's a *monster* down there!"

Tom was surprised by his word choice, but he was more struck by the group's blatant indifference to his urgent message. Nobody reacted, nobody moved. In fact, several patients rolled their eyes, seemingly bored and annoyed by his behavior.

"Did you hear what I just said?! IT RIPPED HIS FUCKING LEG OFF!"

Julie looked at Tom, unshaken, and calmly motioned for him to take a seat.

"Well, Tom, that's one way to introduce yourself."

4

MONSTERS INSIDE

"Twenty bucks on Schizophrenia," Vaughn said.

"You're on. I'm going with Substance Induced Psychotic," replied Mo.

Tom couldn't believe his ears. Here he was, warning people about some wild beast downstairs that was ripping apart hospital employees, only to be misdiagnosed by his fellow patients. Frustrated, Tom kicked over a chair and rushed to make sure the windows were secured.

Julie urged Tom to sit down, but there were simply too many hormones pumping through his body. He locked the windows then hurried back to the circle, pacing frenetically.

"That main entrance is bolted shut, right?" Tom asked.

"Yes," Julie nodded. "Now please, Tom. Take a seat. You're disturbing the other patients."

Tom looked around the group.

"You think I give a shit about any of these people?"

Vaughn, Mo, Omar, Roselle, and Julie all shared a look, then gazed up at Tom with disappointment on their faces. Mo glanced over at Vaughn.

"Scratch that," Mo said. "Antisocial Personality Disorder, final answer—"

"Hey, what did I tell you about pathologizing?" Julie interjected. "We don't do that here."

Vaughn and Mo both sank in their seats, looking guilty.

Julie turned back to her newest patient, "Now Tom, I'm noticing you're distressed. All of us here would really like to hear what's on your mind, and who knows, we might even be able to make you feel better."

Incredulous, Tom slid into a seat in the circle, and took on a mocking tone as he looked around at Julie and his fellow patients.

"Hi everybody, pleasure to meet you. My name's Tom, and I just returned from the basement, where a hospital employee was getting eaten alive by some sick, slimy-ass creature that can break through steel doors."

"What were you doing in the basement?" Julie asked.

Sounding like an audience for a live sitcom, Vaughn and Mo joined together in a collective "you're-in-deep-shit" sound of *ooooooOOO!*

Tom glared at them in disbelief.

"Unfortunately Tom, I'm going to have to report that you attempted to leave the premises. That's going to mean an extension of your time here —"

Tom jumped up, "I don't care! Don't you get it! Why doesn't anybody believe what I'm saying?"

Julie remained visibly calm despite Tom's aggressive posturing.

"Tom, I understand that you just got here. But our number one rule is that we need you to remain calm. Now I would be happy to discuss more about what you're experiencing, what these creatures look like to you, and your relationship to them, but if you do not calm down, I'm going to have to notify Dr. Ellison to administer a sedative."

A sedative? Tom was shocked by what he was hearing. *Had everyone gone crazy?*

"You don't want that booty juice, homie. Just ask Ros,"

Vaughn nodded to Roselle, who was lounged in her seat, her chin resting on her chest as a continuous stream of drool dripped from her mouth, soaking her shirt. Her eyes rolled around slowly in her head, and though it was unclear if she could recognize her surroundings, she grunted at the mention of her name.

Tom definitely didn't want to be in that state. Especially not with that creature downstairs. Then again, Tom thought, the doctor *had* to be more rational than these people. Who the hell *were* therapists, anyway? This Julie lady probably didn't even have a Doctorate. His father always said Masters Degrees were middle class at best. Either way, he'd just stumbled upon a way to get to the doctor once and for all — by doing the opposite of calming down.

"Take me to the doctor... before I kill every one of you," Tom said. It was more extreme than he intended, but it was consistent with his approach to basketball; either go big or go home.

Saddened, Julie nodded and gathered her papers. She looked around at the group and addressed the interruption.

"Until I come back, I want you all to sit with how this interaction landed for you. Try to identify what exactly was coming up."

What a bunch of bullshit, Tom thought.

"Hurry up, lady! Or you're all gonna die!" Tom was not much of an actor, but he could tell he was selling it well. Probably because, based on whatever he saw in the basement, it wasn't a total lie.

TOM CAREFULLY FOLLOWED Julie down the hallway towards Dr. Ellison's office. They were headed down the same corridor that Tom had sprinted away from just moments earlier, so he kept his eyes peeled for any creatures.

"For the record, I'm against this," Julie went on, "Sedating people feels like a relic of old world asylum culture. But when they leave me with no security and no nurses, I don't have much of a choice… It's for everybody's safety."

Tom wasn't listening. He was busy thinking about what he would do if that thing came crashing through the double doors at the end of the hall. Probably jump out the window, Tom thought. He'd rather explode on a sidewalk than get picked apart limb by limb. Tom couldn't unsee what happened to the nurse. The memory of it made him nauseous.

They finally reached Dr. Ellison's door, and Tom noticed that the blinds on the small window were closed. Julie knocked softly, but Tom quickly overrode her actions by pounding on the door with his fist.

Finally, the door swung open, and Dr. Ellison stood there, looking flustered. Blood filled his cheeks as he snapped at Julie.

"Can't you see I'm in a meeting?"

"Sorry Doctor Ellison, but we have a client who won't remain calm."

"Ugh, you therapists are useless. One second," he said, before slamming the door in their faces.

A moment later, the door reopened, and Kiki crept out. Her head was down, her shoulders slumped, and she dragged her feet as she slid by in silence. Both Tom and Julie noticed her demeanor, but just as Julie was about to check in with her, Dr. Ellison called out.

"Julie, get in here," he demanded.

In a supportive gesture, Julie placed her hand on Kiki's shoulder, but Kiki immediately recoiled and continued sulking down the hall. Tom thought the behavior was odd. Moments earlier, Kiki had seemed like the most energetic person on earth. When Julie reluctantly stepped inside Dr. Ellison's office, Tom turned back to catch up with Kiki.

"Hey, you okay?"

Kiki paused and lifted her head to look at Tom, and her face was covered with tears. He also noticed her hair was disheveled and untied. Kiki said nothing, but Tom could tell by her expression that she was not the same person who had entered the doctor's office less than twenty minutes ago. Then Tom remembered it was an exit interview.

"They're making you stay longer?" he asked.

Kiki scoffed and shook her head, then continued down the hall.

"Tom, step inside please."

Tom turned to see Julie waiting for him in the doorway of the doctor's office. He glanced back at Kiki who was slumping down the hallway, then decided that she wasn't his problem. So he swung around, marched down the hall past Julie and stepped into the office.

Dr. Ellison stood behind a large desk, in front of a panoramic window with a view of Manhattan, holding a syringe next to an open refrigerator. The office looked different from the rest of the hospital; there were ancient artifacts on his bookshelves, Herman Miller leather chairs that he recognized from his father's study, framed degrees from Johns Hopkins, Harvard, UC Davis, and a large mirror that the doctor was currently using to tuck a stray nose hair up into his nostril. Without looking at Tom, Dr. Ellison spoke.

"I heard somebody's having trouble controlling themselves. I've got something here that'll do the trick, since our in-house therapist's mindfulness techniques seem to have failed once again. Now, I urge you not to make this difficult."

The doctor squirted liquid from the tip of the syringe and flicked it with his middle finger, when Tom slammed his fists down on the desk, making the doctor jump.

"My name is Tom Walton. I'm the son of Senator Chester Walton of New York, and you need to get me out of here."

Dr. Ellison looked at Tom, intrigued. The doctor glanced up at Julie, who wore an expression of mixed distaste and belief, then motioned for her to leave. Speechless, Julie shook her head and left, shutting the door behind her.

Dr. Ellison turned to face Tom and placed the syringe down on the desk.

"You know, we're taught to never believe patients around here. But saying you're related to the most despised man in this entire borough makes me think you aren't making it up."

"I suggest you take my word for it," Tom said. "Or he'll make sure you never work again."

Dr. Ellison chuckled, seemingly humored by the threat.

"Ah, like father like son. It's a pleasure to meet you Tom. Have a seat."

Dr. Ellison sat down, but Tom remained standing.

"Just call my dad and get me out of here."

"There's a power outage," the doctor replied. "The phone lines are down."

Tom nodded to an iPhone laying on the doctor's minimalist desk.

"Use that."

"I'm not supposed to use personal phones for professional use. It's against protocol."

"Then give it to me and I'll make the call."

"Can't do it, sorry. But I'd be happy to listen to more career threats."

The doctor flashed a toothy smile, relishing in the sudden power shift.

Tom held the doctor's delighted gaze, then lunged forward to try and grab the doctor's cell. The doctor quickly snatched it away, laughing.

"Give me the fucking phone!" Tom yelled.

"Feisty young man! You remind me of myself when I was younger."

Tom didn't know exactly how he felt about that, but he certainly didn't feel good. That's when he noticed Kiki's bright yellow hair tie on Dr. Ellison's wrist. Maybe Kiki hadn't only been robbed of her release, Tom thought.

"Why were the blinds down?" Tom asked.

"I'm sorry?"

"On your door. You pulled them down when Kiki came in."

"Patient confidentiality," Dr. Ellison said, a sinister grin on his face.

Tom held his stare and nodded solemnly. It was clear to them both that there was an accusation being made that could never be proven. But this was someone else's problem, Tom thought. He reminded himself that the reason he came into this office in the first place was to escape this hellhole.

"Please, if you call my father, I guarantee he'll make sure you're taken care of," Tom said.

Dr. Ellison leaned back in his chair.

"That sounds terrific, and I intend on doing so," the doctor said, glancing at his watch. "But I've got a reservation at Nobu in thirty minutes. By the time me and my dungeon mistress finish up with dinner and playtime, it'll be around midnight. So I need you to hang tight until then. Write down your father's number, and I'll give him a ring."

The doctor slid a pen and pad over to Tom, and Tom was met with an unfamiliar burning in his chest. He couldn't tell if it was from feelings of injustice, or because for perhaps the first time, he wasn't getting his way. No, wait a second, it was because there was a freaking monster in the building that he swore to God was real.

"Listen to me. I know it sounds insane, but there's some... thing in the basement that's already killed at least one person."

"Some... *thing?*" Dr. Ellison looked curious.

"I saw it. It wasn't human. It was some... creature."

"*Creature?* Wow, you actually belong here, huh? Who would've thought, a boy of your pedigree with schizophrenia? Ha, I'm gonna make a fortune, let me tell you."

"What are you talking about?"

"Could you imagine how much fun *The Post* would have with this?" The doctor motioned to an imaginary headline in the air, *"'Senator's Son is a Schizo.'"* Delighted, he looked back at Tom, "I hope your father's treasure chest is as deep as he says it is."

Tom couldn't believe the doctor was thinking about money at a time like this. He could feel his adrenaline starting to pump again.

"You need to get us out of here!" Tom demanded.

The doctor put his feet up on the desk, looking thoroughly entertained.

"I know your father's a narcissistic prick, but that's typical of politicians. I take it your mother was the true nutso?"

Suddenly, Tom lunged over the desk and grabbed the doctor by the throat. But Dr. Ellison was deceivingly quick and powerful for his age — he swiftly maneuvered out of the choke hold, picked Tom up, and slammed him down onto the floor. Tom landed on his back, and with the wind knocked from his lungs, he looked up at Ellison, who was choking him with ease.

"You don't work in a place like this without knowing Krav Maga," Ellison chuckled. Still pinning Tom, Dr. Ellison reached up onto his desk and grabbed the syringe.

"Now, I understand you tried to go AWOL. Normally, that's an automatic fortnight. But if you behave yourself, I might do you and your daddy a favor and get you out of here in a couple of days. Capiche?"

Turning purple, Tom nodded.

"Take a breath and relax," Dr. Ellison said. He loosened his grip slightly and Tom gasped for air. "By the time you come back from this, it'll already be Tuesday."

Dr. Ellison moved the syringe towards Tom's leg. Tom struggled in vain, kicking and squirming, and with the syringe's needle just inches away from being plunged into Tom's body, an ear-piercing, unearthly shriek shook the room.

EYES WIDE WITH BEWILDERMENT, Dr. Ellison released Tom and turned towards the interior of the building.

"What in the *world?*"

Dr. Ellison carefully approached the door and peered through the little window out into the corridor. Tom scrambled to his feet, terrified.

"I've heard a lot of women scream in this place," Ellison said. "But that one sounds like she needs a higher level of care."

Just as Dr. Ellison grabbed the door handle —

"Don't open that door," Tom pleaded.

Dr. Ellison turned, humored by the dread in Tom's voice.

"They're just hood rats, son," Ellison said, flicking the syringe. "Besides, I'm locked and loaded."

The doctor winked at Tom, then opened the door and stepped out into the corridor. Tom had been around many people with sociopathic tendencies, but this guy was taking it to a whole new level. Tom watched the doctor step out into the hallway.

BOOM! The sound of metal banging. It was similar to the noise Tom heard in the basement, and when he saw Dr. Ellison turn towards the locked double doors, Tom feared the worst. The doctor laid eyes on something peculiar, furrowed his brow, then stepped out of Tom's view. In the distance, Tom could see Julie rushing down the corridor towards them, flanked by Mo, Omar, Vaughn, and the rest of the patients at Four West.

"Doctor Ellison? Is everything alright?" Julie shouted down the hall.

Tom crept towards the door and peeked his head out to find the doctor standing in the middle of the corridor, staring at the locked double doors.

"Did Roselle get out again?" the doctor asked.

Julie glanced over her shoulder, and saw Roselle shuffling behind them.

"No, she's with us."

Julie and company arrived at the top of the T-shaped corridor, and followed the doctor's eye line to the doubled doors on their left.

The emergency lights illuminating the hallway ended at the double doors, leaving the door windows ominously black. But there was a deep dent in one of the doors, with a unique imprint that featured what looked like claw marks.

"It's not human," Tom said.

Julie and the others looked back at Tom, who was stepping out of the doctor's office to join them in the hallway.

"We need to go before it breaks down that door," Tom urged as he started backpedalling down the hall.

BOOM! Everyone turned to look at the steel door, which now had a second huge dent.

"Doctor Ellison... What is that?" Julie's voice was shaking.

Doctor Ellison was staring at the door, deep in thought, when he calmly turned to Julie and waved her off with a smile.

"Oh, it's just that new janitor," he said, as he started back towards his office. Julie and the others remained in place, looking skeptical.

"What new janitor?" she asked.

Looking suspiciously composed considering the circumstances, Doctor Ellison reached his office and turned to face the group.

"He was all disgruntled about low wages or something..." he said, as he stepped inside the office.

CRASH! Everyone turned to see a something break through the door's glass window. A long, black claw was perched on the window frame, bending the metal with superhuman strength. It was most certainly not a human limb.

"Oh my God," Julie gasped.

"'The fuck is that!?" Vaughn shouted.

Freaked, Julie cried out, "Doctor, what do we do —"

SLAM! Julie turned around to find Doctor Ellison bolting shut the door to his office. The group stood there in disbelief, coming to terms with the fact that the person who was ultimately in charge of their well-being and recovery had just abandoned them. Now they all turned to Julie.

BOOM! Another dent. Julie and the group took a collective step backwards. *BOOM!* The doors were coming loose at the hinges. Tom, who was the furthest down the hall, took another step back, when he suddenly tripped over the halogen construction lamp that was providing the corridor's only light. It crashed to the ground, and the hall was suddenly drenched in darkness, with the exception of a sliver of light that emanated from the far away rec room. Nervous screams echoed through the hall.

"Everyone okay?" Julie asked the group.

"Sorry... I tripped." Tom said, sitting flat on his butt.

The sighs of relief were audible.

"Let's all just stay calm. Everything's going to be fine," Julie said. The uncertainty in her voice was palpable, and her doubts were confirmed when another bone chilling shriek filled the corridor. From the darkness, Omar immediately called out —

"That don't sound *fine* to me."

CRUNCH! The double doors were blown aside, and whatever lurked in the darkness was now charging towards them. Tom picked himself up and started to run.

Tom ran suicides five times a week at basketball practice, so he was near the front of the pack that was sprinting down the hall back towards the rec room. When one of the patients let out a scream that was louder than the rest, Tom could tell it was the type of scream that could only be produced by torturous pain. So Tom ran faster.

Vaughn was the only person ahead of Tom, and when Vaughn turned left at the rec room and headed towards the well-lit dining room, Tom mindlessly followed. He knew nothing about Vaughn or his decision-making skills in life-threatening situations, but he figured they had to be better than his own. Vaughn crossed into the dining room, then stopped short and jumped up to grab a strap that was hanging from the ceiling on one side of the entrance. He turned to Tom and pointed towards the opposite side.

"Grab that one!" He yelled.

Tom slowed and looked up, confused.

"What? What for?!"

Blood curdling screams filled the corridor behind them.

"Just do it yo!"

More horrific screams. Whatever was happening down the hall was something that Tom wanted no part of. So he jumped up, grabbed the strap, and on his way down, he pulled a metal grate down a few inches from the ceiling. Now he understood.

"Once they're all in, we're slamming it closed!" Vaughn yelled at Tom, who nodded in response.

"This way!" Vaughn screamed at the crew as they poured into the rec room and hooked a left into the dining room. Mo and Omar rushed inside, followed by Julie, whose face was dotted with specks of blood from the ones who didn't. As soon as she reached the threshold, she turned.

"HURRY!" She yelled towards the rec room, which was curiously empty and quiet. A good chunk of the patients were still out there.

Everyone listened close, but immediately wished they'd covered their ears, when another monstrous shriek rang through the halls. They recoiled from the sound, then spotted Roselle in the rec room, crawling on all fours.

"Ros, over here!" Julie yelled.

Ros seemed to be moving in slow motion, her motor skills still impaired from the sedatives, as she strutted like a tired cat on her way towards the dining room.

"Come on!" Vaughn yelled.

Before Tom could react, Vaughn released the gate strap and ran out into the rec room towards Ros.

"What are you doing!?" Tom yelled, knowing he'd need Vaughn's strength to pull the gate down. Tom and the group watched helplessly as Vaughn grabbed Ros by the arm, and in one motion lifted her from the ground and tossed her up over his shoulder. He was chugging it back towards the open gate, when Tom noticed something moving on the other side of the rec room. Big Blue, the puffy recliner, was rocking back and forth. Although it was facing the other direction, Tom could see a head adorned with giant headphones bopping gently. And Tom knew it was Kiki's.

Without thinking, Tom bolted past Vaughn and Ros and into the rec room.

"Where the hell you going!?" Vaughn yelled at Tom.

Tom slid over the ping pong table, the way a wheelman slides across the hood of his getaway car in an action film, and landed behind Big Blue. He yanked the headphones down to Kiki's neck, and she jumped up and turned around, fists cocked.

"Oh you did NOT just kill my vibe —-"

A piercing shriek sent a terrified Kiki recoiling from the sound, and when Tom turned, he caught a glimpse of what he could've sworn was a mangled human body being flung through the air — and into the construction lamp that was illuminating the rec room. The lights popped and exploded with sparks, and when Tom saw the silhouette of a creature making its way down the hall towards the rec room, he reached out to grab Kiki's arm —

But she was gone, already ten steps away, sprinting towards the gate. *Oh yeah, this isn't a movie,* Tom thought. The sparks from the construction lights suddenly died out, drenching the rec room in darkness. The creature shrieked violently and Tom kicked it into high gear.

Back at the gate, Vaughn unloaded a moaning Roselle to Julie, then jumped up and grabbed the strap. Kiki quickly crossed the threshold, then turned around to scan the darkness for Tom.

There was no sign of him.

"Tom!?"

The monster shrieked again, and it sounded like it was closer than ever. Finally, Tom shot through the dark, jumped up to grab a strap, and with Vaughn's help on the other side, they used their all their weight to yank the gate to the ground, when —

BANG! As soon as it hit the floor, they were both thrown back by a creature crashing into the gate. Landing on their asses several feet inside the dining room, Tom and Vaughn looked at each other, stunned. Unable to make out the creature hissing at them in the darkness, Tom grabbed Julie's flashlight and pointed it at the gate.

A glimpse is all Tom got, when the bloodstained orifice of some hideous beast let out a painful screech so loud that he dropped the light. The flashlight rolled over to Mo, who quickly picked it up and kept aim on the creature that was suddenly retreating into the darkness.

"I think it's scared of the light!" Mo exclaimed.

"Then keep shining that shit!" Vaughn yelled.

The creature disappeared from their line of sight, and Mo kept the light steady on the gate that was responsible for saving their lives. They caught their breaths, all shaking, all horrified, and when Tom looked around at them and started to open his mouth, Vaughn cut him off —

"Say '*I told you so,*' and I'll open this gate right now and feed you to them things."

So Tom just thought the words instead.

5

LIGHTS ON

"So… when did this hospital begin treating aliens?" Kiki asked to no one in particular. Everyone looked to Julie for the answer, who was at a loss for words as she wiped someone else's blood from her eyes.

"This is really happening, right? I mean, you guys didn't accidentally mix up our medications or something?" Mo asked.

Julie showed everyone the blood on her shaking hands.

"Looks pretty real to me," she said.

"There's some guy on my block who breeds dogs and other animals in his garage," Omar said. "Maybe it's some kind of crossbreed of like… a pitbull, a cockroach, and a lightning fast crackhead from the eighties."

Vaughn climbed to his feet, "You're all buggin'. We're not high, and that thing isn't an alien or some kinda dog-roach. It's some kind of biological weapon the government created to exterminate people of color."

"What about me?" Tom asked.

"What *about* you? As far as I know, you brought that thing in here. None of this started going down until your white ass showed up," Vaughn said, his eyes like daggers. Tom averted his gaze, knowing there was at least some truth in Vaughn's statement.

"Relax, Vaughn," Kiki said. "If it wasn't for Tom, I would've gotten my head ripped off during a musical interlude. And that's just depressing."

Tom looked at Kiki, and although the light within her looked relatively dim, he could see that she genuinely appreciated him.

"Tom don't give a damn about any of us," Vaughn said. "He straight up said it in group therapy."

Tom tried to defend himself, "I didn't mean that though —"

"The only reason he saved you," Vaughn cut him off, looking at Kiki, "Is because he's trying to smash. You know how I know? Because Roselle was stranded out there on all fours, about to get eaten by that thing, and he didn't move a muscle. But when he saw you, homie grew wings."

"That's not true," Tom disputed. "You just looked like you had it under control with Ros."

"Don't play with me," Vaughn said, as he stepped closer to Tom. "I see right through that selfish bullshit. You would leave us all to die if it meant saving your own ass, just like Doctor Ellison. Matter of fact, I bet y'all roll in the same circles... Where you from, anyway?"

Uh oh.

Tom could feel the whole crew staring at him, and he started to turn red. This was a disadvantage of being white, he thought. Embarrassment sucked for everyone, but at least people with darker skin didn't also have to worry about turning into a tomato.

"Alright boys, that's enough!" Julie said.

Tom was suddenly grateful for Julie's presence. She went on, "Now is not the time for this crap! We need to focus on the present predicament, which is that we are currently on the fourth floor of a decrepit hospital, inside a cafeteria with no exits and no phone lines, hiding from some bloodthirsty creature that'll rip us in half if we try to leave."

The group sat in silence, taking that in. Tom looked up at the windows on the back wall.

"Do those open?" Tom asked. Not waiting on a response, he jumped up, hustled over, and began cranking the lever on one of the casement windows until it swung open six inches.

"What are you going to do?" Julie asked.

Suddenly, Tom took a deep breath and screamed out the window, "HELLLLLLP!" Tom could hear it echo through the dark alleys below, until it slowly faded away.

"Pshh" Vaughn scoffed at Tom and looked to the others, "This dude is lost."

Tom ignored the comment and took another deep breath, stuck his head back into the window opening and yelled again, "HELP US!" Once again, Tom listened to his voice ricocheting between the adjacent brick apartment buildings, until the cascading echo dissipated into silence. He desperately scanned the sidewalk below, which was illuminated by the occasional orange street light, but was perplexed by the lack of activity. There were no people, no cars. The block was deserted.

"You forget where you're at, bro?" Omar asked.

Tom turned away from the window, looking puzzled.

"You must be hella stressed," Omar said. "'Cause we all know damn well that ain't nobody chilling outside after dark in this part of town."

Tom tried to play it off with a shrug. He realized his actions were likely to reveal the fact that he was from a neighborhood where people packed diners and bars until four a.m. on weeknights. He glanced out the window one last time, then sauntered back towards the others.

"Also, this is the psych ward," Mo said. "I highly doubt you're the first person to scream for help from one of these windows."

"I can confirm that he's not," Julie chimed in. "Honestly, the people living around here are probably so habituated that your screams are actually helping them sleep."

Tom sat down on a plastic chair near the rest of the group, dejected.

"Lullaby Scream," Kiki muttered. "That'd be a great song title."

"Hell yeah, that sounds like a DMX song," Omar said with a smile, then added, "He would've killed something like that... R.I.P."

The others nodded and cast their eyes downward. Tom looked around and could tell that their love and respect for the deceased rapper was real. Tom wasn't all that familiar, but he liked that one party song about losing one's mind "up in here," and he appreciated the fact that he seemed quite fond of dogs, but he just couldn't understand why people paid tribute to the dead in general. Dead people were gone; it wasn't like they could hear anyone's well-wishes.

The group shared a moment of silence.

"So... anybody got any *good* ideas on how to get out of this place?" Vaughn asked.

Tom didn't like Vaughn's not-so-subtle dig at his failed escape plan. But it was still better than what anyone else had thrown out, Tom thought.

"Maybe we should just stay here and hang out," Tom responded, with a smart-alecky tone in his voice.

Vaughn immediately *psshhh*-ed the notion.

"I think Tom's right," Julie said, to everyone's surprise. "If what Mo said about the light is true, then we're safe in here, for now. There's only one way out, and our chances of survival don't look so hot if we try to escape past that thing. We've got food for days in the kitchen back there, so I say we wait it out until help arrives."

"What makes you think somebody's coming to help us?" Vaughn asked, motioning to Tom. "Did you not just watch this kid scream out the window?"

"Doctor Ellison is a slimy piece of garbage, but he's the only one allowed to have a cell phone on him at all times, and I guarantee he's already called for outside help," Julie responded.

The group considered the idea, and a consensual nod made its way around the room, ending with a reluctant Vaughn. With that, Julie climbed to her feet and began collecting empty chairs.

"What are you doing?" Mo asked.

Julie dragged the empty chairs deeper into the cafeteria, towards an area that was dimly lit by a pair of emergency light boxes that were fixed to the ceiling. She positioned the chairs into a circle, as the group of patients looked at her like she had truly lost her mind.

"Well, we'd might as well make the most of our time," Julie said.

She sat down in one of the chairs and waved the others forward.

"The healing must go on."

Tom, Vaughn, Mo, Kiki, Julie, and Omar sat in a circle in the cafeteria, underneath the dull emergency lights, which had presumably kicked on at the start of the blackout.

They stared at each other in deafening silence.

"The floor is open to whoever would like to begin," Julie said.

The group stayed quiet, but everyone seemed to be waiting on Tom. Except for Roselle, of course, who was resting on the floor in a sedated sleep.

"Don't look at me. I don't even know how this works," Tom said.

"You talk about what's your mind, that's all," Julie explained. "You're safe to speak freely here, and nothing is off limits."

"Okay, um... if I'm being totally honest, I think you're batshit for wanting to do therapy at a time like this."

Julie nodded, "It sounds like you feel angry and frustrated

because you disagree with the way I'm handling this situation. Is that right?"

"Yeah, I guess," Tom said.

"Just making sure I'm understanding the way you feel. Now regarding this situation, how would you prefer I was handling it?" Julie asked.

Tom shrugged, "I don't know. Figuring out other ways to get the hell out of here. Crawling through vents or swinging out the window on fire hoses." Tom knew it sounded ridiculous the moment he said it.

"Okay, Tom Cruise," Vaughn cracked, earning a chuckle from Mo and Kiki.

"Vaughn, please," Julie gave Vaughn a chastening look, who abided with a nod. Julie turned back to Tom, "So you'd prefer if I was helping us escape?"

"Anything but sitting here! I feel like the goat from *Jurassic Park*, just waiting to be fed to the freaking dinosaur," Tom cried.

He wasn't trying to be funny. And he wasn't trying to make non-stop movie references, but films were the closest he'd ever come to experiencing danger that wasn't self-initiated. That was their favorite pastime, him and his mom. They would take turns choosing the film for movie night, and Tom could still remember the night his mom chose *Jurassic Park*. The movie blew his mind, despite being made like a hundred years ago. But the days of movie nights were long gone; the only time Tom watched movies these days was when he felt too lonely to sleep.

"Being here is scary, no doubt," Julie said. "I think we all would agree with that."

Tom's mind returned to the room, and he looked around at nods from the group.

Julie leaned in close and said, "I think everyone here would also agree that running from what scares us can often make things worse." Julie was peering into Tom's eyes, "And that includes our emotions."

Tom scoffed and shook his head, humored by how corny and cliché this whole process seemed. But when Tom scanned the expressions of his group members, he was shocked to find them looking open and tuned in.

Julie continued, "I wonder if your desire to avoid those uncomfortable and scary and sometimes even painful emotions, might have contributed to why you're here with us at Bronx Memorial today."

She was good, Tom thought. Like Robin Williams in *Good Will Hunting,* without the doctorate, of course.

"Do you want to tell us why you're here?" Julie asked.

Tom squirmed in his seat. He knew that if he told his story, he'd have to leave out certain details about his identity given his audience, and he hadn't really thought it through yet. So he shook his head.

"Would it be helpful to hear from someone else first?" Julie offered.

Tom really didn't care to know more about the others, since he had no intention of staying connected with them once this nightmare came to an end, but he was happy to shift the attention onto somebody else. Tom shrugged, *sure.*

"I'll go," Mo said, without hesitation. "I'm here because I love books."

Tom looked confused. He scanned his group members' faces, and judging by their lack of reactions, they'd all heard this story already.

"You're here because you love *books*?" Tom asked, double-checking.

Mo sat up tall and gave a proud nod. "Yup, ever since I was little," she said. Mo cleared her voice and went on, "My father was locked up for most of my childhood, so I was raised by my mom. She was on drugs and all that, so she would disappear for days at a time, leaving me at home with nothing to eat. We lived in my grandma's apartment in Soundview, and my grandma was there for like fifty years before she died. Anyway, she held on to every book she ever read. So whenever my mom left me at home, I just stayed inside and read every single book she had on those bookshelves. Probably four hundred books. All before I was ten years-old."

Tom looked confused by what the problem was, "That sounds like a healthy habit. My dad says that if... people read more books on their own, we wouldn't have to worry about a broken education system."

The comment got some curious glares from the group. Julie, in particular, gave Tom a knowing a look. Tom remembered that Julie had overheard his true identity during his interaction with Doctor Ellison. Thank goodness for client confidentiality, Tom thought.

"Right, the reading is healthy, but..." Mo shifted uncomfortably. She looked down at her feet, ashamed, "There was no food in the fridge, and nothing in the cabinets, so..."

Tom furrowed his brow, trying to figure out where Mo was going with this.

"I ate every page I ever read," she said.

Tom must not have heard that correctly.

"Did you say *ate*?" Tom asked.

"Now Tom," Julie interjected. "Let me remind you, there's no judgment allowed in here."

Mo shrugged at Julie, as if to say, *it's no big deal.*

"I'm not judging," Tom lied. "I'm just... surprised. I've never heard of anyone doing that."

"Big Pun ate his walls," Omar said. "True story. Nicest lyricist of all time, but he had issues for real. His step-pops used to beat him and he'd be stressed or whatever, so he would eat chunks of drywall in his bedroom."

"*Dead in the middle of Little Italy little did we know,*" Vaughn did his best Big Pun impression. As he finished out the famous line,

Omar joined him, "*That we riddled some middlemen who didn't do diddly!*" Omar reached across the circle to give Vaughn a pound.

"Pun was nasty!" Vaughn said.

"Put Puerto Rico on the map, son! For real," Omar sat back down. Tom knew of Big Pun, but he'd never heard those lyrics before. He wanted to hear more.

"Omar, what are the rules about interrupting?" Julie asked.

"That's my bad. I just wanted to boost Mo a bit, you know. Tell her about somebody who had them same issues, but became a legend," Omar said.

"Thanks Omar," Mo said.

"No doubt. But go on, sis. My bad for cutting you off."

"Basically, that's the story. I started doing it 'cause I was hungry, you know. I just wanted something in my stomach. And paper was better than air... But even once my mom got a job and started putting food on the table, I kept doing it. Eventually she caught me. The only book my mom ever opened was her King James Bible. She read it every day. But once I got through all my grandma's books, I couldn't help but nibble on that King James. So she kicked me out... I've been living on the streets since, hanging out in libraries after school. Was all good until the cops caught me at the library on 168th street, finishing up the Young Adult section."

Tom didn't know what to say. He'd never even made eye contact with a homeless person, let alone spoken with one. Come to think of it, as far as he knew, this was the first time he'd ever interacted with someone who'd actually experienced the sensation of hunger. In Tom's home, Rosa delivered meals whether he wanted them or not. Feeling overly full was his primary problem.

"Thank you for sharing your story with us again, Mo," Julie said. "Tom, what was it like hearing Mo's story?"

Depressing as hell, Tom thought. But he couldn't say that. What *could* he say? There was nothing in her story that he could relate to, except for the reading part. Then he remembered the religious studies class he took at Manhattan Prep last year.

"So what did you think of the Bible?" Tom asked.

"Hm, tough question." Mo glanced up at the ceiling, deep in thought, then looked back at Tom, "You really wanna know?"

Tom nodded.

"Taste was too bloody for me. I prefer the flavor of Eastern religious texts."

Mo tried to hold a straight face, but the entire group immediately burst out laughing, Tom included. Julie chuckled, looking proud of her group's developing rapport, when the flashlight that was shining on the dining room gate suddenly went out.

The laughter died, and everybody turned towards the darkness.

"Dammit Mo, why'd you have to talk shit about God?" Omar asked, before a hoarse, ear-splitting screech tightened the knots in their stomachs.

VAUGHN HURRIED towards the dark drenched gate and knelt down to grab the flashlight. He smacked it a few times, but it was totally dead. He turned back to the crew.

"We need to find another light—"

BOOM! The creature crashed into the gate and shrieked as Vaughn jumped back to join the others in the middle of the dining room.

Thinking fast, Tom grabbed a chair and pushed it up against one wall.

"Get that side!" he yelled out, motioning to the emergency light fixtures that were lining the ceiling on each side. Vaughn was already on it.

Tom climbed on top of the chair, reached towards one of light fixtures, and tried angling it towards the gate. But the weak beam didn't quite reach.

The creature banged against the gate again, undeterred by the dim lights. Vaughn tried to angle the second set of lights in the same direction, but they were also too far from the gate to make a difference. The creature was shaking the gate, and the sounds of crunching and clanging metal sent Vaughn back into survival mode.

Suddenly, Vaughn grabbed the light fixture, and with all his might, he ripped the fixture clear off the wall. Dry wall came tumbling down as Vaughn jumped down from the chair and flashed the light towards the gate — and immediately sent the creature retreating into the darkness. Vaughn kept the beam directed at the gate, as the others gathered behind him.

Everybody breathed a sigh of relief, until they noticed a slit down the middle of the gate. The creature had managed to saw straight through the metal grating.

Tom hopped down from his chair, and stepped closer to Vaughn to get a better look at the damage.

"Looks like those push-ups paid off," Tom said to Vaughn. Tom nodded to the light fixture that Vaughn had just ripped from the wall. It was Tom's way of saying thanks for saving our lives, without having to thank someone who clearly despised him. Vaughn looked down at the fixture in his hands, and rather than responding to Tom, he frowned.

"Ay yo, I don't know much about electricity, but if this thing is still working after I just ripped it from the wall..." Vaughn looked up at Tom, confused. There was a hint of fear on his face.

"There must not be a back up generator," Mo called out from behind them. "All these emergency lights are battery operated."

"Battery operated?" Tom asked. "How long do they last?"

Mo rushed over to the light fixture in Vaughn's hand, and leaned in close to inspect the back of it. The others waited in suspense.

"Uh oh," Mo said. "Anyone know when the lights first went out?"

"Around eight P.M." Julie replied.

"And what time is it now?" Mo's voice was shaking.

Julie checked her watch, "Nine fifty."

"So that leaves us…"

Mo performed the calculations in her head, and the group waited in nervous anticipation, until suddenly, her eyes went wide.

"Ten minutes."

It took less than *ten seconds* for the group to be divided.

"This is our only chance to get out of here alive," Vaughn said, before he marched back behind the cafeteria's kitchen counter.

"What are you talking about?" asked Julie.

"That thing's scared of light," Vaughn said. "So I say we use these lights while they still got ten minutes of life in 'em and get the fuck outta here."

"I said the lights went out at *around* eight," Julie said. "So I don't know for sure how much time we've got. Could be ten minutes, could be two."

"Even more reason to hurry," Vaughn pushed through the double doors leading to the kitchen.

"Where are you going?" Julie asked.

"To get some weapons," Vaughn said, as he disappeared into the kitchen.

Julie turned to face the rest of the group, and she could see that all of them were unsure of how to respond. They listened to the sounds of Vaughn banging his way through kitchen drawers, until finally, Kiki shook her head.

"I need to get out of here," Kiki said. "I'm done with this place."

Julie looked both surprised and disappointed. Tom did a quick assessment of the situation. Something about weapons felt smart, and his current company didn't give him much confidence.

Tom averted the gazes of Julie, Omar, and Mo, and hurried towards the kitchen.

"I really don't think you should do this," Julie said, but Tom and Kiki had already pushed through the doors into the kitchen.

Julie turned towards Omar, Mo, and Roselle, who was still resting on the floor, half asleep.

"What do you guys think?" Julie asked.

Omar and Mo were shaking their heads.

"Doctor Ellison gave me hella Xanax earlier," Omar said. "So I'm moving in slow motion right now. And Roselle is toast, son. Ain't no way we gonna outrun some alien carrying her big ass around."

"What do you think, Julie?" Mo asked.

Julie paused to think, "What we've been doing seemed to be working. As long as we can find another light, I think waiting it out is our best bet."

Mo nodded in agreement, "We're in a commercial kitchen for Christ's sake. I'll figure out how to create light."

Mo rushed towards the kitchen, and Julie and Omar shared a hopeful look.

Just as Mo was about to push through the doors, Vaughn emerged, flanked by Tom and Kiki. Vaughn held a meat cleaver in one hand, and a roll of duct tape in the other. Kiki carried a cast iron pan with both hands, and Tom held a pair of steak knives, one in each hand.

Mo stopped to look at her warrior colleagues and shook her head, "You guys think you're gonna fight that thing?! If it can cut through a metal gate, it's gonna bend those freaking knives in half."

Tom thought she had a point, but he was swept up in the confident energy of Vaughn and Kiki. Now was not the time to express doubt.

Vaughn put his weapons down, pulled a chair towards the

wall, and swiftly ripped another light fixture from the dry wall. He handed it off to Tom and tossed the duct tape to Kiki.

"Tape that onto his chest," Vaughn said. When he saw the reluctant looks of Tom and Kiki, he explained, "You need free hands to use weapons!"

Kiki looked at the tape, then quickly got to work, taping the fixture tight to Tom's bare chest, which was still exposed from his ripped shirt. Tom was worried sick about the mission that they were about to embark on, yet he couldn't help but enjoy having Kiki so close to him. Although she touched his body in a way that was anything but sexual, he could feel his heart rate increasing. And it had nothing to with the fact that he was potentially only seconds away from getting his insides ripped out by some monster. She smelled so damn good, Tom thought.

"My turn," Kiki said, as she slapped on the last piece of duct tape onto Tom's back. Kiki grabbed the fixture that Vaughn had ripped from the wall and held it in place on her chest. Tom quickly grabbed the roll and criss crossed the tape over her shoulders, and around her sides. Tom couldn't believe how sticky duct tape was. He'd heard about people using it to fix things, but he'd never actually had to do that. When things broke in his house, they threw them out. Fixing things was for poor people, his dad would say. Tom hated the way his thoughts worked. Why was he thinking that kind of stuff in a moment like this? He was taping up a beautiful young woman, whose hair smelled so much like rosemary that it could be used for aromatherapy, in attempt to escape from a hospital that's been invaded by —

"That's enough, dude!" Kiki snapped. "Jesus."

Tom hadn't realized he'd been taping her excessively while trapped in thought.

"Sorry," he said. Tom ripped the tape and turned to Vaughn, who had already ripped another light fixture from the wall. Tom stepped towards Vaughn, ready to help him get strapped, but Vaughn threw his hand up.

"Don't touch me," Vaughn growled. He snatched the duct tape from Tom's hand and started taping it up himself. Okay, Tom thought. Not like I wanted to smell your hair too.

Tom grabbed his knives and stepped closer to the gate to join Kiki, who was taking deep breaths with her eyes closed, holding the cast iron pan in her hands.

"Guys," Julie called out from behind them, "I'm saying this as your friend, and not your supervisor. *Don't do this.*"

"For real," Omar said. "Yo Vaughn, you realize if those lights turn off, y'all are gonna be assed out."

Vaughn ignored the warnings and joined Tom and Kiki at the threshold. The lights fixed to their chests shot three white beams into the darkness beyond the gate. Their weapons glistened at their sides.

"Y'all ready?" Vaughn asked them. Tom shrugged and nodded at the same time. No one can be ready for a moment like this, Tom thought. Kiki remained still. Her eyes were closed, but her lips were moving. She was praying silently.

"Please," Julie put her hand on Kiki's shoulder. "What you're doing is reckless. We can barricade ourselves in the kitchen and buy us some more time," Julie pleaded.

Kiki turned and opened her eyes, which were overflowing with tears. Julie looked surprised and worried.

"Time is out of my price range," Kiki muttered.

Julie took this in, and a look of sadness washed over her face as she came to realize what was being communicated. Disheartened, Kiki turned back to the gate. Tom heard the interaction, but it didn't feel like the right time to inquire about subtext.

"Ready?" Kiki asked.

"Y'all should get back," Vaughn called over his shoulder to the others.

Julie and Omar quickly gathered up Roselle, and as Mo led them into the kitchen, she shouted back to others, "If you make it out, send help!"

"We will! Love y'all!" Kiki said.

"Love you too!" Mo yelled back.

Once the kitchen doors swung closed, the dining room fell silent. Looking determined, Kiki nodded to Vaughn and Tom.

"Let's boogie," Kiki said.

Together, Vaughn and Tom reached down and lifted the gate.

THEY SLAMMED the gate closed behind them.

The trio carefully approached the rec room, white knuckling their weapons, when Tom realized a weakness in their plan.

"Hold on," Tom said. They all froze. "We need to move back-to-back or we're leaving our rear exposed." Tom didn't know anything about actual combat, but every time his grandfather, who was a WWII veteran, climbed into their family's Lexus SUV, his grandfather made sure everybody knew that the Japanese liked to shoot people in the back. So did the Americans, his mom would say, and then all hell would break loose for the entire road trip out to Montauk. Tom resented his mom in many ways, but sometimes he wished more of her badass traits would've rubbed off on him. Instead, here he was, trembling with fear, one fart away from crapping his pants.

Vaughn and Kiki nodded, and they switched formations so that they moved together in a tight triangle. The light fixtures strapped to each of their chests now illuminated all sides of them. Tom took up the rear, and crept backwards, away from the dining room.

They crossed the rec room, which was still and eerily silent. Where the hell did that thing go, Tom wondered. The only thing he could hear was the sound of their hurried breaths, when Kiki suddenly gasped.

Tom started to turn around to investigate —

"Stop!" Vaughn snapped. "Keep the lights steady."

Oh, right. So Tom resumed the position, and whispered, "What is it, Kiki?"

Kiki was facing the corridor they'd rushed down during their initial escape, but it looked a whole lot different now; blood decorated the walls and ceilings in a series of smears and splatters, and a dark red river stretched down the length of the hall and past Doctor Ellison's door, the window of which was somehow still illuminated. The most shocking part of the grisly scene was the sheer absence of bodies.

"They're all gone," Kiki sounded horrified.

"Maybe they got out," Tom said hopefully.

"They didn't," she said.

Tom swallowed in fear. Part of him wanted to see for himself what had happened to the patients whose names he'd never learn, but he knew it would probably make his legs weak. And he needed his legs now more than ever.

"We gotta move faster," Vaughn said.

They picked up the pace and moved towards the entrance to Four West, when Vaughn's lights shined on the double doors through which Tom had first arrived.

Vaughn stopped, "Shit! We forgot to grab the key from Julie."

How could they forget something like that? Tom was angry at himself for mindlessly tossing the lanyard with the plastic key card back to Julie after his adventurous bathroom trip. He barely remembered doing it; that moment was such a blur. *This sort of thinking isn't useful,* Tom thought. *We need to think of a Plan B.*

Kiki looked panicked, "We're running out of time."

"We gotta go down the other staircase," Vaughn said.

"No way," Tom responded. "That's where I first saw that thing. For all we know, that's where its nest is or whatever."

"So what if it is? That's why we got these lights on us," Vaughn sounded like he was getting agitated.

"And if the lights shut off?" Tom asked.

"Now is not the time to start acting scared," Vaughn barked as he whipped around, ready to lay into Tom —

"Stop, Vaughn! Keep the lights pointed out there," Kiki yelled.

Vaughn quickly swung back, when a loud shriek tore through the corridor. It sounded like it was coming from beyond the double doors in front of them. They instinctually began retreating into the rec room, scanning the environment for any sign of movement.

"Listen," Vaughn said to Tom. "Kiki and I are going down the back staircase. It's the only other way out. So either you're coming with us, or you can sit here and play ping pong with your new monster friend."

Tom knew it was decision time. Although he was worried about the lights going out, he still figured he had a better chance of surviving as long as he stayed with Vaughn. Vaughn had gotten them into the dining room safely. That was more than anyone else had done.

Tom heard a strange hissing sound echo through the rec room.

"Did you guys hear that?" he asked.

"Yeah, you see anything over there?" Kiki responded.

Tom shifted left and right, his lights revealing nothing but pieces of rec room furniture. He called over his shoulder to Kiki, "Nothing."

"All clear over here," Vaughn said. "Let's move."

As soon as Vaughn took a step towards the corridor, a cacophony of ungodly hisses and shrieks filled the rec room, when suddenly, his lights flickered and went out. The noises stopped, and the hallway in front of them was suddenly cast in darkness. Vaughn cursed and smacked the light fixture on his chest, but it was toast.

"My lights are dead!" Vaughn yelled as he used the meat cleaver in his hand cut the duct tape from his chest. The light fixture dropped to the floor.

"Kiki, you get the front," Vaughn said as he stepped behind Kiki. Kiki turned her body to illuminate the corridor up ahead, when the creature flashed across the end of hallway, escaping the light beam.

"There it is!" Kiki screamed.

Tom instinctually turned to look, but then remembered to guard the rear. When he turned back, he saw something flash across the rec room past the Big Blue chair.

"It's over here now!" Tom yelled.

"That's impossible," Vaughn said, as he turned to inspect the rec room over Tom's shoulder.

"It was near the recliner, right over there!" Tom's voice cracked, before continuing, "Maybe there's more than one of them." As the trio pondered this terrifying possibility, Tom and Vaughn were staring into the stillness of the rec room, when Tom's lights suddenly conked out.

"Uh oh," Tom said.

"What is it?" Kiki asked, as she remained focused on the corridor.

"All we got is your lights," Vaughn told her. "WE NEED TO GO NOW!"

"But it's gonna be right behind us!" Tom shouted. "We need to go back!"

Vaughn turned to Kiki, who was frozen in place. Her lights were beginning to flicker, the battery power slowly waning.

"Kiki, either start moving, or gimme those damn lights!" Vaughn yelled, just as a combination of strange hissing and clicking sounds began filling the rec room once again. Vaughn slowly craned his neck and looked up at the ceiling.

"Oh my God," Vaughn whispered, in a fearful tone. "Get back in the dining room."

Tom and Kiki turned to Vaughn, who was already backpedalling, eyes fixed to the ceiling. All of a sudden, Vaughn spun around and bolted back towards the gate. Confused, Tom and Kiki turned to see what Vaughn had spotted, and Kiki's lights flickered on for a second to illuminate the ceiling, where a mass of undulating dark bodies, each one the size of an adult bear, scattered like cockroaches.

Tom hated the fact that he was right; there *was* more than one creature.

The shrieks and hisses sent Tom and Kiki reeling backwards, and they began racing back towards the gate, the creatures giving chase. Kiki's lights flickered on and off to create a strobe light effect, and the combination of chaotic flashes along with the soundtrack of ghastly cries from the merciless beasts produced an atmosphere fit for a night club in hell.

Up ahead, Vaughn had reached the gate, where he was ready and waiting to slam it down as soon as the others crossed the threshold.

Kiki and Tom bolted towards the gate as the creatures closed in. The bouncing light beams from Kiki's fixture were helping to stall their being attacked, until finally, they went out. Kiki, who was a step or two ahead of Tom, ripped the dead light fixture from her chest to lose the extra weight. When it dropped, however, Tom immediately stepped on it, turned his ankle, and face planted on the floor.

Kiki rushed past the gate, and Vaughn started to yank it down. Kiki whipped around to see Tom climbing to his feet, limping on one leg, with one of the creatures quickly emerging from the darkness behind him —

"Wait!" Kiki yelled at Vaughn, who halted the gate at the halfway mark.

Kiki dashed back out into the rec room, and Tom spotted her coming. Tom couldn't understand why she was running back into the danger zone, until he watched her grab the light fixture off the floor, pick it up, and swing it mightily at the creature who was only seconds away from pouncing on Tom's back. The creature reeled and retreated, but there was another one coming. Kiki turned and pushed Tom forward towards the gate, sending him flying forward onto the slippery floors. He scrambled underneath the gate, and Kiki dove under.

Vaughn slammed the gate closed, just as a pack of creatures crashed violently into the gate. Pieces of concrete began falling from the ceiling as gate's structure was being compromised.

"It's not gonna hold them!" Vaughn screamed.

Suddenly, an explosive orange light burst forth from the cafeteria behind them, sending the creatures retreating back into the darkness.

Vaughn, Kiki, and Tom turned to figure out what had just saved their lives, and were relieved to find Mo, Omar, and Julie standing at the cafeteria food counter, in front of a dozen chafing dishes filled with nothing but bright orange flames.

Mo stood near the check-out counter, behind a bevy of flammable chemical products she'd collected. A lighter in one hand, and a can of Lysol spray in the other, she pointed the can at one of the blazing chafing dishes, and squeezed. An explosive burst of orange light shot into the air, and Mo smiled, like a proud chef working a hibachi grill.

In a lordly voice, Mo proclaimed, "And Mo said, Let there be light!" She chuckled, then sprayed another explosive burst.

"And there was hella light."

6

STOKE THE FIRE

Everybody sat around the cafeteria counter, which had become a makeshift campfire emitting bright chemical flames, as Vaughn shared the bleak updates: there was more than one creature, there was no sign of survivors, and they were all in very deep shit.

Tom winced in pain as he used a piece of his ripped shirt to wrap his ankle. He'd turned his ankle plenty of times in basketball practice, but this was the first time he'd used duct tape to keep it all secure. Tom couldn't believe how useful the stuff was.

"You okay?" Kiki asked.

Tom looked up at Kiki who took a seat on the floor next to him.

"Yeah, just twisted it," Tom said. An uncomfortable silence filled the space between them as Tom tried to figure out how to express his gratitude. He couldn't understand why it felt so difficult, but he had to say something.

"Thanks," is all he could manage to squeeze out.

"For what?" Kiki asked.

Tom thought it was obvious, but he clarified, "Knocking the crap out of that thing. I'd probably be dead if you hadn't come back to help me."

"Without a doubt," Kiki replied. "But I owed you one." A smile on her face, Kiki lifted her arm to offer up a fist bump, and Tom awkwardly met hers. He'd never fist bumped a girl, he thought. Fists were things you bumped with friends. According to his dad, women weren't supposed to be your friends. Not unless you were one of those musical theater kids.

"You think a lot, huh?" Kiki asked.

Tom was surprised by the accuracy of her question, as he was already knee-deep in the memory of he and his mom watching The Juilliard School's rendition of the musical *Once*. Whenever they went to shows, Tom's mission was to procure more tissues in order to soak up his mom's tears. But Tom could remember her blowing through more than ever that night. That was right before everything went south. Looking back, Tom wondered if her tears had anything to do with *Once* at all.

Tom remembered that Kiki had said something.

"Sorry, what'd you say?" He asked.

Kiki chuckled, "Your mind wanders."

"Oh. Yeah, sometimes," Tom responded, downplaying the severity of his own ADHD, which he often did. He knew so many kids in school who faked the diagnosis just so they could get some extra time on exams, and he hated those kids. Tom didn't want Kiki — or anyone — to think he was one of them.

"I used to be that way," Kiki said. "But then I realized that you can get so in your head that you lose touch with the ground."

Tom's curiosity was piqued.

"Want to know the secret to staying sane?" Kiki asked, looking eager to share. "Depression lives in the past. Anxiety lives in the future. So if you keep your mind rooted in the present moment, neither one of them can get you, because the past and future don't exist in the now."

Tom nodded as he considered the idea. He'd never heard it put that way. Then again, depression and anxiety sounded marvelous compared to present predicament of being hunted by flesh eating monsters.

"No offense, but the present moment sucks," Tom said.

"Does it, though?" Kiki motioned to their surroundings. "Right now, in this very moment, you're safe. Things are okay. Your heart is beating. Your lungs work. You can walk. Sure, the moment you step outside that gate, those beasts might end up playing soccer with your head, but if you're living your entire life worried about what's going to happen next, what's the difference? Not like you were ever really alive anyway."

Tom was busy taking that in, when the sounds of slow clapping stole their attention. Tom and Kiki looked up to find the others facing them and applauding, and it became clear that the group had been watching and listening to their entire conversation. Mo and Omar were sharing a bag of popcorn that they'd found in the kitchen.

"Couldn't have said it better myself, Kiki," Julie said, looking proud.

"I thought y'all was gonna kiss, but that's because I ain't had access to *Pornhub* in like four days and that's just where my heads at," Omar said.

The group chuckled, and Kiki playfully jumped up to punch Omar. Tom remained on the floor, thinking about what it would be like to kiss Kiki. But then he remembered they were fist bump friends. Kissing was off the table.

"I'm glad y'all are having a good time," Vaughn barked.

Everyone turned to face Vaughn, who looked deadly serious.

"I ain't happy about what just happened," he said. "We had a chance to get outta here, but y'all two were too shook to move."

"What are you talking about?" Tom replied, "You're the one that ran back here first."

Vaughn picked up the meat cleaver and rushed at Tom. Vaughn stopped short, standing above Tom, holding the blade directly in front of his face.

Tom did his best to remain still.

"Vaughn, put that down, now!" Julie yelled.

Tom looked up at Vaughn, "Sorry man. I didn't mean anything by it... I'm obviously a little screwed up to be in a mental hospital to begin with."

Vaughn peered into Tom's eyes, assessing for bullshit.

"Vaughn, take a deep breath," Kiki said. "The problem is outside that gate, not in here."

Vaughn pressed the end of the blade into Tom's forehead, not quite hard enough to draw blood and said, "Watch yourself. I've got zero patience."

I can tell, Tom thought. But he didn't dare say it.

Vaughn lowered the meat cleaver and returned to the counter, where he sat down and stared into the flames. Tom exhaled with relief, having survived his first ever experience of being threatened with a deadly weapon by someone other than himself. He'd held knives to his own throat before, especially after his mom died, but he never intended to go through with it. His dad didn't pay Rosa enough to clean up that sort of mess.

Mo and Omar, who were still sharing a bag of popcorn, nodded to one other, put the snacks down, and began arranging the cafeteria chairs in a circle. The others watched them with dubious expressions.

"What are you guys doing?" Julie asked.

"We've got enough flammable liquids to last us at least another two hours," Mo said, as she excitedly jumped into her seat. "So we'd might as well pick up where we left off."

A proud smile grew on Julie's face as Omar fell into the chair next to Mo.

"This group needs healing, Julie," Omar continued, "Shit's mad obvious."

"Who'd like to go next?" Julie asked, surveying the room.

Tom watched Kiki join the circle and take a seat. Nothing

about this makes sense, Tom thought. But since he didn't have any better ideas, Tom slid over and plopped down in a seat.

Nobody volunteered to speak. They looked around at one another, and noticed that Vaughn was still brooding at the cafeteria counter.

"I think Vaughn's got some stuff he needs to deal with," Omar said. Vaughn glared at Omar, but Omar continued and nodded at Tom, "Especially after scaring the piss outta our newest guest. Changed this dude's complexion from manilla envelope to Casper the ghost."

Kiki and Mo snickered. Tom couldn't help but smile. Tom had never heard jokes about his skin color before. But if there were jokes about other races, Tom thought, there had to be white ones too. Skin color was something Tom never had to think about growing up. There was some talk about critical race theory being taught at Manhattan Prep, but all the parents who paid the hefty tuition swore they'd pull their children out of school and move to Idaho before that ever happened. Tom didn't really know what it was, nor did he give a shit.

"Yo, I just had a wild thought," Omar's voice was filled with excitement. He looked at Tom, "I bet you prolly be like, camouflage when you walk into a bathroom. Like if people broke into your crib, and you didn't want nobody to find you, you could just get naked and sit on the toilet."

Even Vaughn chuckled at that, as the tension in the room dissipated.

"I'm happy to hear some laughter from the group, but I want to check in with Tom," Julie chimed in, with a caring look on her face. "Is any of this offensive? How are these jokes landing for you?"

Tom shrugged, "I don't really mind —"

"You can't be serious," Vaughn scoffed, visibly agitated with Julie. "We really sitting here and checking in about the white guy's feelings?"

Omar jumped in, "Yo, we got a few white boys in school with us over at Clinton, and I'ma be honest with you... there's one or two that are straight G's, but the rest of them, they get bullied like a mofo. Kids be slapping their cheeks to see how purple they can get 'em and what not. One of them's liable to shoot up the school one day. Dead ass."

"Yeah, but that's only in the Bronx," Vaughn said. "Go anywhere else in the world, and white people be the ones doing *all* the bullying."

"That's irrelevant, homie," Omar said. "You invalidating Tom's individual experience right now. Tom is a Bronx white, which means that on the inside, he's more like... cream colored or whatever."

Omar looked at Tom, feeling good about giving a voice to what he assumed was Tom's struggle. Tom, however, was turning red with embarrassment. He glanced up at Julie, who was looking at Tom with curiosity, assessing how Tom was handling this mix-up about his identity.

"A Bronx white is different from Connecticut white, nahmean? I hate them Cape Cod, sailboatin' white people too, but he ain't one of them. If he was, he sure wouldn't be here with us at Bronx Shithole Memorial."

Omar turned to Tom, "Am I right?"

Tom's mouth went dry. And before he could think, he felt his head starting to nod. When he looked up, he saw a hint of disappointment on Julie's face. He kept staring at her, wondering if she was going to reveal his secret to the group, but that wasn't a therapist's job.

"Tell us about yourself, Tom," Julie said.

"Um...," Tom muttered, as he shifted uncomfortably in his seat.

He tried to think of the names of schools and neighborhoods in the Bronx so that he could fabricate his story, but he couldn't come up with anything. Nobody in his circles knew anything about the Bronx except for Yankee Stadium, the Bronx Zoo, and that it was where you woke up with no shoes and no wallet if you passed out on the Uptown trains.

"I was just like you when I came in," Omar said to Tom. "Scared of being open about my experience. But it feels good, son. Which is why I'm cutting you off and going next... if you're cool with it, of course."

Tom shrugged, concealing how desperately he wanted someone else to talk. Omar looked at Julie for permission, which she granted with a nod.

"So out there, I'm a pusher. Molly, crack, coke, oxy, all that. Whatever you need, I got it, right? I started selling to help out momdukes, cause when she got out of jail, she couldn't get a job —"

"How old are you?" Tom asked.

"Fifteen, was twelve when I started hustling," Omar said.

Tom was shocked. The hardest thing Tom had to deal with at the age of twelve was saying goodbye to friends on the last day of summer camp.

"Anyway, I'm hustling, and making so much cake that momdukes don't need to get a job. And she starts experimenting with my product, you know. They be going hard with the pills at Rikers, so she already had some experience. I told her to chill, because I'd be coming home finding her passed out sometimes, and I seen what those pills can do to people. But she's my mom, you know, so I wanna make her happy. Eventually, we even started doing some of it together. I'd cut school and we'd just throw on some Drill shit and get outta our minds...," Omar chuckled at the memory, but his smile slowly faded. Eyes cast down at the floor, he went on, "Moms was wild. She was my best friend for real... But then one day I came home from school... and found her dead on the sofa."

Omar sniffled and looked up at the group with tears in his eyes. He smiled and shook his head, "Shit still gets me, yo."

Julie reached over and put her hand on Omar's knee.

"We're here for you," Julie said.

Omar cleared his throat and took a deep breath, "Long story short, I felt mad guilty about what happened. Still do. If I wasn't selling drugs, my mom might still be around. She died of an overdose... and it's my fault."

A wave of emotion came over Omar, and he doubled over in his chair. He hung his head between his legs and began sobbing uncontrollably, hiding his face from the rest of the group.

"Ahhh, shit *still* gets me!" Omar yelled.

The group sat there in silence, as Omar wiped tears from his eyes. Tom felt a strange sensation in his chest, and could've sworn his eyes were getting watery. Tom fought the tears back as Omar sat up.

"Anyway, I know about what happens to kids when they lose their only guardian. They either become part of the system, or they can live that street life forever. And I didn't want either of those things." Omar pounded his fist into his sternum and said, "So I stabbed myself in the chest."

"Jesus," Tom muttered, not realizing he said it out loud. Omar glanced over at Tom, who suddenly felt obligated to say something else. "Wait, so what happened... when you stabbed yourself?"

To everyone's surprise, Omar cracked a smile.

"I didn't tell the rest of y'all this part, but..." Omar cleared his throat, glanced around at the group, and then delivered the kicker:

"The pencil broke."

"You tried to kill yourself with a *pencil?*" Tom asked, with a tone of disbelief that was so honest, it was unintentionally funny.

Omar burst out laughing, and the others joined in.

"Hold up. A wood pencil or one of them mechanical joints?" Vaughn asked.

"Straight wood, bro," Omar said through his own laughter.

"You gotta be careful when you high! I got it in a few inches, but then the shit snapped off and I was like damn, I ain't getting this out by myself. Walked my ass right over here, lifted up my shirt and told the receptionist I lost my pencil."

More laughter filled the room. Tom looked around at his fellow patients, and the joy on their faces intrigued him. Especially Omar's. Maybe Omar was right; maybe there really was something that felt good about being open.

"My mom died too," Tom said.

The laughter quieted down as everybody turned their attention to Tom. *Nope, Omar was wrong,* Tom thought. *Nothing feels good about this.*

TOM SUDDENLY FELT like he'd reached the top of a rollercoaster about to make its descent, and he desperately wished he could stop the ride. He didn't mind talking about himself in front of groups; he just wasn't used to editing stories in real time for any details that might reveal he was a Walton.

Keep it short, Tom thought. *Less margin for error.*

"My dad was never around, 'cause he was always working..."

Omit the type of work he does, Tom thought.

"Mom was unemployed, so since she was home all the time, we were pretty close..."

Omit the fact that dad insisted mom quit her job as a schoolteacher because it looked bad politically, claiming that the wives of powerful men didn't work.

"She drank quite a bit, and my parents would fight about money, mostly..."

Definitely omit the fact that mom couldn't understand dad's desire to hoard more money when they already had so much of it. Omit the part about mom just wanting them to spend more time together as a family.

"Anyway, she started going to bars all the time. Then one day,

I came home from school and found her hooking up with some bartender."

"Oh damn. Your mom was a golddigger?" Omar asked.

Tom looked confused.

"Omar, please—" Julie started to reprimand the interruption.

"No, no, it's okay," Tom said. He looked at Omar, "What do you mean?"

"It's obvious," Omar said. "Bartenders make mad dough. Your pops wasn't bringing home that bacon, so she found somebody who could."

That's *crazy*, Tom thought. Bartenders were broke-ass bums where he came from. In fact, when Tom's mom told his dad about the affair that night, she claimed that the young bartender's nonchalant attitude towards money was one of the reasons she sought him out. Tom could still remember overhearing their conversation. It was gross and painful but he couldn't help but listen from the hallway. His mom claimed that she actually felt a connection with the young man, and felt "seen" for once in her life. When she told Senator Walton that he made her feel dead inside, his father didn't seem too upset about it, and so Tom assumed they were both dead inside.

"Something like that," Tom responded to Omar, knowing that his mom was the opposite of a gold digger.

"So what'd you do when you found them?" Vaughn asked.

Tom shook his head, "I flipped out... And called her a whore."

The shift in Tom's voice caught everyone's attention. He sounded like he was getting choked up. Because he was.

"Damn son. You said that to your own mom?" Omar asked.

Tom nodded solemnly.

"What else was he gonna say?" Vaughn asked, seemingly defending Tom. "*Keep up the good work, mom?* Hell no. Don't get me wrong, you should never disrespect your mother, but Tom said exactly how he felt. He kept it real, and I respect that." Vaughn gave Tom a commending look.

"Freakin' New Yorkers, man," Mo said. "Always bragging about how direct they are, but there's a difference between being direct and being hurtful. Keeping it real isn't an excuse to be mean."

Vaughn scoffed at Mo, dismissing her comment.

"How do *you* reflect on what you said, Tom?" Julie asked.

"I agree with Mo," Tom said. Vaughn turned to him, looking surprised, so Tom explained, "The next day, they found her car upside down on the FDR drive. She got drunk and flipped over the median."

Oh shit. That was the look on everyone's face.

Tom's eyes were glassy, "It was the last word I said to her."

"So that's why you jumped into the river?" Kiki asked.

Tom hung his head, hiding his tears from the rest of the group. When Kiki reached over and put her hand on his shoulder, he lifted his head and looked around at his group members. He felt supported. He felt connected. He felt *seen*. He also felt like he was learning a thing or two about how to lighten things up when a room felt too heavy.

"It was a hot night," Tom shrugged, "I just wanted to take a swim."

Chuckles filled the room. *Phew*, Tom thought. He'd gotten through it without lying, for the most part. Just a few minor omissions here and there.

"It ain't your fault your moms died, you both know that right?" Vaughn said. He was looking at Omar and Tom, "It's the system's. The reason your moms were out of work to begin with. The reason people in our communities feel the need to escape using drugs and alcohol. The reason we're forced to do questionable things to get outta poverty. The system ain't designed for people like us to thrive."

The group sat quietly, digesting Vaughn's words. Tom loved the sound of "people like us," but he knew he was a fraud. He pretended to be on board, nodding his head and avoiding Julie's gaze at all costs.

"Word," Omar said, seemingly gaining some insight from Vaughn's comments. "You know in kindergarten how they ask you to draw a picture of what you wanna be when you grow up? It ain't like I drew a paranoid stick-figure dude in his underwear, sitting in his kitchen stuffing powder into baggies. It was just the only option to get real cake aside from robbing people, but I ain't got the heart for that."

Vaughn nodded at Omar in solidarity.

"This system is twisted," Omar said. "Gets me so heated."

"You have no idea," Vaughn said.

Tom noticed Vaughn was clenching his fists, and Julie must have seen the same thing.

"Vaughn, I'm noticing some tension in your body," Julie said. "What's coming up for you right now?"

"Nothing," Vaughn replied, but he was clearly unnerved.

"I know we've been trying to get Tom to talk, but we haven't heard Vaughn's story either," Mo said.

Kiki agreed, "Yeah Vaughn, let's hear it. It's not like we've got anything else to do but wait for the cops to come."

"Pshh, the *cops*," Vaughn said. "You wanna hear a little story about *cops?*"

Vaughn scooted his chair closer, and jumped right in, "Couple days ago, my mom was trying to get me ready for the driver's test. So we borrowed my neighbor's car and took it to the C-Town parking lot late at night. The place was totally empty, so we switched seats and I was doing my thing, you know. She was teaching me to put my hands at ten and two and all that, but I kept one-handing it at midnight like a straight G..." Vaughn smiled, reminiscing.

"All of a sudden, we see those red and blue lights. Cop car pulls up behind us. I stop the car. My mom tells me it's alright, 'cause I got a learner's permit and all that, so I'm chilling... But the cops come up, both white, and they both got their guns drawn. They tell me to put my hands on the wheel, so I do it. They start asking me questions about insurance and registration and shit, but I don't know the answers because it ain't my car... My mom tries telling them what the deal is, who the car belongs to, and they see that she's wearing her nightgown. We weren't going nowhere but to practice driving, you feel me. And the cops keep shining the lights on her legs and shit, not listening to what she's saying..." Vaughn cleared his throat and balled up his fist, his body getting tense.

"Then one of them asks me to turn the car back on, and put on Hot 97. I'm sitting there like, what kind of shit is this? But I do it, 'cause they still got their guns out. Then the same officer tells me to roll down all the windows and turn the radio up. So Peter Rosenberg got some French Montana shit blasting on the radio, when one of the cops popped the passenger side door open. My mom wasn't going nowhere, until the cop said, 'You and your son are driving a stolen car. But we'll let you off the hook if you do something for us.'"

Vaughn was grinding his teeth and avoiding eye contact with the group, visualizing the story with so much intensity it seemed like he was about to burn a hole in the floor.

"They told my mom to get out, brought her to the front of the car so that she was lit up by the headlights... and told her to dance."

Vaughn's voice cracked upon uttering that last word. When Vaughn looked up at the group, anger and pain tried to escaped through his flaring nostrils. Vaughn wasn't crying, but he had every right to, Tom thought. Tom felt like he'd been punched in the gut.

"I was ready to kill one of them," Vaughn said, "But as soon as I hopped out the car, they started hammering me with those nightsticks... They cuffed me up, shoved me back into the car and made me watch her dance. Thank God they didn't take it any further than that. My mom just danced the lamest Macarena she could until the cops got bored and left."

"Damn," Omar said as he shook his head.

"I'm so sorry that you experienced something like that," Julie said.

"I would've killed them," Tom said.

His comment surprised everyone, except for Vaughn.

"That's why I'm here," Vaughn told him.

"You... *killed* them?" Tom was shocked. He wouldn't *really* have killed them.

"Na, but as soon as my mom and I got home, I promised my mom I was gonna get 'em. She was begging me not to, but I went on YouTube, and found some videos on how to build a bomb. I built that shit in no time, crazy how fast you can learn when you're motivated... I was headed over to the precinct, ready to blow a hole in something, when my mom saw the websites pulled up on my computer. She called it in... I got scooped up before I could light the fuse."

"Honestly, I would've done the same thing," Mo said.

"Me too," Omar agreed. "Freaking cops, bro."

"I bet if you did a study measuring average dick size, and analyzed differences between occupations," Mo said, "You'd find that cops fell several standard deviations below the mean."

Chuckles filled the room.

"I'm serious," Mo said. "Little dick energy is a threat to humanity. I read that Hitler had a micropenis... that's a fact."

Tom had never really thought about that. He wondered about his father's junk size, and remembered back to when his father was first teaching him how to pee into a toilet. Tom could recall his dad's junk looking slightly bigger than his at the time, but he was only a toddler. Come to think of it, Tom was absolutely certain he'd outgrown his father. What a profound revelation. Tom didn't know where his line of thinking was taking him, but he was pretty sure that the last twenty seconds of zoning out during an alien invasion was solid evidence that he truly *did* need his monthly prescription for Vyvanse.

Tom's attention shifted again, this time to subtle flashes of red and blue lights that he spotted on the ceiling.

"What's that?" Tom pointed up.

Everyone looked, then turned to the windows, where flashing emergency lights were ricocheting off an adjacent building. Tom could hear the sounds of police sirens in the distance.

"The cops are here!" Mo yelled, as she jumped up and ran to the window. The others followed right behind, pressing their foreheads against the glass windows. Down below, they could see a pair of police cars about a block away, coasting down the street towards the front of the hospital.

Omar pounded on the glass, "Up here, you little dick mother-fuckers!"

They'd cranked open several windows and were screaming at the top of their lungs to try and signal for help. The two white and blue police cars were about half a block away, when they slowed to a steady crawl...

"What the hell are they doing?" Tom said. "Don't slow down!"

Everybody yelled louder.

But the cop cars crept to a stop.

BLURP-BLURP! The sirens yelped, and suddenly their spotlights turned on, but they were pointed towards the sidewalk on the opposite side of the street. The lights illuminated a homeless man urinating on the side of a liquor store. Another homeless man was seated on a plastic crate, holding a bottle of booze in one hand and shading his eyes from the blinding lights with the other.

The group was coming to terms with the grim reality of the situation; the cops weren't there for them. They were there to protect the one booming business in the area.

"Are you serious?" Vaughn seethed. "Who gives a damn about some dude pissing?" Vaughn leaned as far out the window as he could get before screaming, "AY YO THERE'S PEOPLE DYING UP HERE!"

His voiced bounced off the brick building across the street, but whether it reached the street or not would forever be a mystery.

Three police officers were already upon the two homeless men, and when the one who was urinating started to run, he was quickly tackled to the sidewalk. The officers laughed and cheered the cop who made the tackle, and even hi-fived like the defensive squad of a high school football team.

One of the cops took the homeless man's bottle of booze, shattered it on the ground, then grabbed him up off his crate. The two homeless men were thrown into the back seat of separate squad cars, and the cops hopped back into their vehicles.

Acting quickly, Vaughn spun around and picked up a chair from the cafeteria, then turned back to the windows.

"Get out of the way!" Vaughn yelled.

Tom and the others stepped back, and Vaughn lifted the chair above his head, then slammed it into the window with all his might.

But it didn't even chip the glass.

The chair bounced off and sent Vaughn stumbling. Although his attempt failed, everyone liked the idea. They had to get the attention of the cops if they wanted to leave this hospital alive.

"Grab the table!" Julie screamed. She rushed to grab one of the heavy cafeteria tables, with Vaughn, Omar, and Kiki helping to pick it up off the ground.

Tom peered out the window, and could see the cops had shut their siren lights off. The cars began speeding down the block towards the front of the hospital.

"HURRY UP!" Tom screamed.

When he turned around, his group members were already

rushing the window with the table in hand like a battering ram. Tom dove out of the way when —

THUD. The table crashed into the glass window, sending the batterers tumbling into each other, but the sound of impact was disappointing. Tom checked the damage and saw that they managed to crack the window, yet the glass was too thick to break through.

"God dammit!" Julie yelled.

Tom was panicked. He needed to do something. Anything. The police — despite the things they did to Vaughn and his mom, and the way they just tackled that homeless guy with his junk out — were sworn protectors of citizens of New York City, and Tom had faith they'd put their lives on the line to save theirs if given the chance. He needed to give them that chance.

Tom looked around desperately, when he spotted an emergency fire lever on the wall inside the cafeteria. He'd seen the same ones in school, and remembered back to when he and Westley pulled it once during gym class, sick and tired of doing burpees at eight a.m. after a night of champagne enemas. From what he understood, those alarms made a ton of noise and notified the police automatically.

Tom rushed back into the cafeteria, as the others watched him, confused.

Mo leaned against the window and looked down, "They're getting away!"

Finally, Tom reached the lever, smashed through the plastic casing with his elbow, then yanked it down.

Tom was thrilled to see a flashing red light on the ceiling strobing on and off in conjunction with a blaring alarm crying, *BERP... BERP... BERP...*

Semi-hopeful, everybody swung back to the windows, only to see the squad cars drive directly past the front of the hospital before disappearing around the street corner. The group turned around one by one, looking deflated.

"Guys, it's okay," Tom said, trying to lift spirits. "These alarms are linked to emergency systems, so the cops will know for sure that something's wrong here."

"Let it go, bro," Vaughn said. "Nobody's coming to help us."

"Tom?" Mo asked cautiously, as she squinted over Tom's shoulder "My eyesight is crap, but what does that say right above the fire alarm?"

Tom turned and saw a large engraving on the wall that he had somehow overlooked, and it spelled a word that filled him with dread:

SPRINKLERS.

A strange rumbling emanated from the walls. Pipes clanked and banged, and the fire sprinklers lining the ceilings started to hiss.

Tom turned back to the group, eyes wide with terror.

Oh no.

PSHHHH! Water began spraying down on them with the strength of a tropical storm. Everybody instinctually scrambled to the cafeteria counter in a desperate attempt to shield their only light source, but there was nothing they could do...

Within seconds, the fires went out.

Full of panic and remorse, Tom looked at the group, whose faces were now cast in darkness, when the ungodly shrieks returned.

Vaughn cocked his head to the side, inspecting Tom with a puzzled look.

"Ay yo... what is that?" Vaughn asked.

Tom was confused, until he noticed that the sudden darkness had revealed the glowing red substance covering his clothing and skin from head to toe. The pulsating continued, and it seemed brighter than it was back when he first discovered it in the bathroom.

"THE SCENT IS ON *Him*!"

Roselle had awoken from her slumber, and she was shuffling

towards them from the far end of the cafeteria. She pointed at Tom, her long index finger outstretched like a tree branch. The whites in her eyes practically glowed in the dark, as she proclaimed in a haunting, rhythmic tone:

"No one listens, no one believes.
The reason things happen, goes back to the Beast.
The stories are true, the stories are grim.
The hounds have risen, and the scent is on —"

BOOM! The cafeteria gate came crashing down, and Roselle didn't even have time to scream. Through the blinking red emergency lights, Tom and the others caught a glimpse of Roselle's body being dismembered by a ferocious beast.

And then three more joined the feast.

7

STICKY TRUTH

Vaughn broke for the kitchen, and the rest of the crew followed, with the exception of Tom. It wasn't so much the shocking images of a woman being devoured by savage monsters that froze him; it was the intensity of her claims that Tom was somehow responsible for this mayhem. Tom felt disconnected from his body, like he was an objective observer of some grotesque horror film in which a lonely kid was about to be eaten by giant cockroaches. *What is that kid doing just standing there,* Tom thought. And then the sound of a hideous shriek helped remind Tom that that kid was him, and he suddenly reconnected with his body and got his ass moving.

Tom turned and bolted, sloshing across the wet floors, and pushed through the swinging doors to the kitchen. As soon as he made it through, Vaughn and the crew rolled a giant freezer in front of the doors to barricade the entryway.

"That too!" Vaughn yelled, and only once the red lights flashed on, they could see he was pointing to a tall, metallic storage cabinet.

Vaughn and Omar rushed over and tipped the cabinet over onto its side, its contents crashing all over the floor, then pushed it flush against the freezer. Two lines of defense.

BOOM! The creatures smashed into the doors.

"It's not gonna hold 'em!" Omar yelled.

"Is there any way out of here?!" Mo screamed.

"The service exit!" Julie said, as she rushed deeper into the kitchen. They followed her past the dishwasher and industrial sinks, past the refrigerators, then hooked a left after the giant walk-in freezer. They bolted through the dry storage area, and Vaughn, who was taking up the rear, proceeded to pull down every storage shelf they passed, creating a barricade of steel bars behind them.

The shrieks echoed through the kitchen, and the volume indicated that the beasts had already broken through the door.

Finally, Julie reached an exit door and pushed through the crash bar. It popped open, and the crew quickly found themselves emptying out into the main corridor of Four West. Water was gushing down on them, and blood washed from the walls to form rust colored puddles at their feet.

Down the hall, a light emanated from the window of Dr. Ellison's office. Julie and the crew rushed down the hall and began pounding on the door.

"Doctor Ellison! Let us in!" Julie screamed.

Vaughn peered in through the window, and saw Doctor Ellison standing at the open window of his sprinkler-free office. He was holding his cell phone to his ear, as he shined a flashlight out the window, switching it on and off to signal for help.

"Open the door, you coward-ass punk!" Vaughn screamed.

"Chill bro, that ain't gonna work," Omar said, stepping in front of Vaughn. "Excuse me, Sir Doctor Ellison. You are the most intelligent, most accomplished, and most highly respected man in the entire medical field, and therefore we call on you for your assistance!"

Doctor Ellison turned and looked at Omar, and immediately approached the door.

Omar glanced at the others, looking hopeful, "Yo, it worked!"

Omar turned back to the window, and Doctor Ellison was just inches away, their faces separated by double-paned glass.

"Where's the Walton boy?" Doctor Ellison asked, his hot breath fogging the window.

Tom, who could hear every word, subtly stepped aside to remain out of Doctor Ellison's view.

"What? The *who*?" Omar asked, confused.

Vaughn shoved Omar out of the way again, "Just open the door, man! We're gonna die out here!"

"Is Walton's son with you?" Doctor Ellison inquired again.

Tom wanted to cower and hide away, but he had to play it casual.

Vaughn turned to the others, confused, "What's he talking about?"

Tom knew. So did Julie. But they feigned ignorance and imitated the cluelessness of the others.

"Only certified dickheads be taking attendance during an alien invasion," Omar said.

Doctor Ellison pounded on the glass to get their attention, "Hey! If you want to live, bring me the Walton boy... Otherwise, good night."

Doctor Ellison smiled and suddenly lowered the window shutters.

Omar's hope switched to explosive rage.

"¡HIJO DE PUTA!"

BOOM! The service door from the kitchen was blown off the hinges, and a beast came crashing into the corridor.

"My office!" Julie yelled, as she turned to run.

The group bolted down the hall after Julie, slipping and sliding across the soaked floors, until they reached a steel door. Julie scrambled for her key card, and her trembling hand held the card out in front of the sensor for what seemed like an eternity. Finally, the door unlocked, and Julie shoved it open.

They rushed inside the dry office, and Tom slammed the door behind them. Julie started tearing through her desk drawers.

"Candles! Light the candles!" Julie screamed, as she pulled out a box of matches. She struck a match and, hands shaking, began lighting a series of tea light candles that she had scattered around the office on top of bookshelves and filing cabinets. Everybody lit a match of their own, and rushed to light the room. Within seconds, the dark office resembled a flickering vigil, and Julie worked to arranged the candles near the door's window to repel the beasts.

They blew out their matches and stood in a circle, catching their breaths.

"So..." Kiki said. "Who the hell is the Walton boy?"

"Julie, you know everybody's last name in here, right?" Mo asked.

They all turned to Julie, who was staring into space, looking at no one in particular as she considered her options. Gradually, her head began to nod, as if she'd come to a complicated, but definitive decision.

"I'm not allowed to breach confidentiality unless a client is a danger to themselves, or a danger to others," Julie said, much to Tom's relief. "But given our current circumstances, that client's decision to keep his identity a secret might be robbing the rest of us of our only chance at getting out of here alive."

Julie looked up and locked eyes with Tom. Tom's stomach dropped to the floor, and when the rest of the crew turned to look at him, he felt like vomiting.

"Tom? Your last name is Walton?" Mo asked.

Tom felt betrayed, furious at Julie for outing him.

"Why do I know that name?" Vaughn asked rhetorically, as he rolled through his mental rolodex.

"I don't get it," Omar said. "So you know Doctor Ellison? How come you didn't say nothing when he asked about you?"

Tom shrugged and shook his head, playing dumb.

"SoBro Luxury Housing," Vaughn said. He looked up at Tom, and he could tell by Tom's terrified look that he was right.

The others looked lost.

Vaughn started laughing to himself, amazed at how they'd all been deceived. His laugh took a menacing tone, as he began walking towards Tom, "Our boy Tom here's been holding out on us. His pops is the one that pushed to get this hospital shut down so he could turn it into luxury apartments. His pops is also the one who's been pushing racist-ass policies for years that benefit the wealthy. His pops talks about all the improvements he's made to the public school system in New York City, but sends his kid to private school on the Upper East Side..."

Vaughn was face to face with Tom, "Manhattan Prep, was it?"

Tom couldn't bare to look Vaughn in the eyes, full of shame and fear.

"Nobody ever asked where I went to school," Tom said, his voice cracking like a seventh graders'.

"You mean... you're not a Bronx white?" Omar asked, appalled.

In that moment, Tom truly wished he was.

Vaughn shook his head in anger and disgust, "Nope. He's one of those upper east side, old money, son of a politician, lie to your face whites."

Vaughn shoved Tom back into Julie's desk. Tom almost flipped over it, but he regained his footing as Julie and the others stepped in front of Vaughn.

"Hey!" Julie yelled. "That's not going to help anything. I only revealed Tom's identity because it could save us. Regardless of how backwards it is, the truth is that help will arrive much sooner if they know that the Senator's son is stuck in here with us."

Omar was physically holding Vaughn back. Vaughn jerked one of his arms free and pointed at Tom, "You're lucky I don't throw you out that window."

Tom's heart was pounding. The rage on Vaughn's face was frightening. He'd only seen that sort of anger once before, on the face of the reporter who accosted his father earlier that evening.

"Why do you hate me?" Tom asked. "I haven't done anything to you."

Vaughn stared at Tom, astonished.

"You haven't done anything to me?" Vaughn scoffed. "So four hundred years of physical, psychological, and spiritual abuse was nothing? Preserving a system that helps your people start the game on third base while mine are still trying to get to first. That sounds fair to you?"

Tom was confused, and suddenly really wished he'd paid more attention to that issue about critical race theory.

"So I'm a bad person because I was born white?" Tom asked.

"I'm sure it ain't the only reason," Vaughn said. He took a second to reflect, and realized his anger was spewing out things he didn't quite mean.

"Honestly?" Vaughn wanted to clarify, "You might not even be a bad person. You're just ignorant as a motherfucker."

"Will you guys chill out?" Kiki said. "The fact is that Tom still tried to kill himself. Rich or poor, he's still a human being in suffering."

"You think I give a damn about the emotional problems of rich white kids?" Vaughn asked, incredulous.

"You should," Kiki said. "Unless there's a freaking revolution like this country has never seen, which I would love more than anything, the reality of this broken system is that those rich white kids are probably gonna be running things one day, like it or not. And it's only gonna get worse if all the people in power are out of their goddamn minds."

It was depressingly true, Tom thought. But there was something else irking him. He felt like he was being dismissed as an individual, like he was being viewed as a symbol rather than an actual person. He didn't like how it felt to be pre-judged by the color of his skin.

"We're not *all* bad, you know," Tom said.

"And neither are we," Vaughn snapped back. "The difference is, society believes you."

Vaughn plopped down in a chair as Tom took in Vaughn's words. *Holy shit*, Tom thought, *Vaughn has been pre-judged by the color of his skin for his entire life.* Tom had heard claims about racism being alive and well in America, mostly on channels like CNN and MSNBC. Maybe they weren't just "liberal circle jerks," as his father liked to call them. All media had an agenda, Tom was sure about that, but maybe being concerned about social issues took a deeper level of understanding that people like his father didn't have the time — or the heart — to consider. All of a sudden, Tom wondered if he truly *was* ignorant as a motherfucker.

"My people are suffering," Vaughn said, sounding tired and despondent. "But your people, y'all got the privilege to choose between being part of the problem, or being part of the solution." Vaughn locked eyes with Tom, "I just don't understand why so many of y'all choose to make things worse."

A shriek in the corridor was so loud that it cracked the glass on the door's window. The crew recoiled, realizing they were still in grave danger. Vaughn stood up to peek through the door's window, surveying the hall.

"So what's the plan now?" Mo asked.

Vaughn turned around and grabbed a fat, flaming candle off a shelf, then slid it across Julie's desk over to Tom. He nodded to the corridor.

"The Walton boy's gonna go call his daddy."

Tom gulped, fearful. He looked around at the others to see if they were in support of Vaughn's idea.

"I mean, right now you're kinda like Christopher Columbus to me," Omar went on, pointing to the colorful substance on Tom's clothing, "Bringing your glow-in-the-dark syphilis over here and destroying the Natives. You should've stayed your ass in Europe, bro."

"What does that even mean, Omar?" Kiki asked.

"It means I'm with Vaughn," Omar said. "Tom brought those things here. He also turned the sprinklers on, which is basically the reason why Roselle is dead."

Omar looked at Tom, "Sorry bro. I don't hate you quite as much as Vaughn, but you messed up. If anybody's going back out there, it's you."

Tom couldn't understand how the arrival of unidentified human-eating monsters could be solely his fault, but he'd definitely pulled the lever that resulted in Roselle's death. And it wasn't like somebody else could call his father for him. Resigned, Tom knelt down and began to tighten his sneakers.

"Wait a second," Kiki said. "What *about* that goo that's all over Tom? And what was Roselle talking about? It seemed like she knew those things were coming."

Nobody had an answer. They all looked mystified.

"Told y'all they were hounds," Omar said. "Cockroach hounds."

Suddenly, an idea dawned on Julie. "Her file!" she shouted. Julie quickly pulled open the drawer to one of the room's several filing cabinets. As she thumbed through hundreds of alphabetized folders, she continued, "The day shift therapist left a note saying that I had to read Roselle's notes from today... he didn't know what to make of her hallucinations... he joked about being careful at work tonight because something evil was coming."

"You sure they were hallucinations and not... premonitions?" Kiki asked.

The crew shared a variety of expressions. Mo, Omar, and Julie, looked fretful. Vaughn and Tom, however, appeared skeptical.

"Well, something evil came," Vaughn scoffed as he pointed at Tom. "Roselle had that part right."

Tom bit his tongue.

"You know... the attack *did* happen soon after Tom's arrival," Mo said in a timid voice, "But you know what else it coincided with?"

They all turned to face her.

"The blackout."

"I don't get it," Omar said. "You saying those things came down from outer space and caused the power outage?"

"I'm just theorizing, dude. I don't work for NASA," Mo said. "But maybe they aren't aliens the way we think of aliens. Maybe they don't come from outer space. Maybe they come from right here."

"Like... from underground?" Vaughn asked.

"It would make sense," Mo replied. "Considering their fear of light... I'm no expert, but I literally just read a book about insects banging. If you ask me, those things are behaving like cicadas. Or aphids."

"How so?" Kiki asked.

"Some cicadas remain dormant for up to seventeen years, then they come out of hiding to mate... and that stuff on Tom could either be pheromones or excrement, both of which are used to mark paths to rich food sources for the rest of their brood..."

"You're saying there's more coming?" Tom asked.

Mo shrugged, "It's not uncommon for some species to scout the environment first, to ensure the survival of their offspring."

The crew silently digested the huge implications of this state-ment, when —

WHAM! Julie slammed a thick folder on her desk, opened it up, and spread around dozens of papers covered in violent draw-ings and chicken scratch. The crew began inspecting the papers, looking for anything helpful. Kiki began reading aloud, "*Client was discovered on the bank of the Harlem River near 145th Street with a grenade launcher. When police officers asked what she was hunting, she told them that 'the hounds were coming back,' and asked for their assistance. She told them that she had a "box truck full of deadly pies" in case the hounds got past her, at which point she was detained. Client refused to disclose location of the alleged truck, and investigators deemed her claims were not credible."*

Everyone looked at Kiki, confused.

"One-forty-fifth street," Tom said. "That's where I jumped off the bridge... and landed in this red stuff."

"Wait, so you *knew* you had that stuff on you?" Vaughn asked, looking for clarification. "So when the hounds showed up and started trying to kill us, you didn't think it was worth mentioning?"

Tom shrugged with guilt. The contempt on Vaughn's face was clear.

"It doesn't matter anymore, Vaughn," Mo said. "We're here now."

"Back up," Omar said. "Roselle said the hounds were 'coming back'?"

Kiki double checked the document and nodded.

"That means they've been here before," Tom said. He turned to Mo, looking impressed, "Your cicada theory might be right."

Mo didn't know how to respond, since it wasn't exactly good news.

"I found them!" Julie hollered. "The day therapist's progress notes."

Julie skimmed the page, then read aloud: "*Client denies existence of any auditory or visual hallucinations, and reports that she is one of a select group who are actively fighting evils conjured up by 'The Curse.' Client sports an 'X' tattoo on the back of her hand that she claims is a symbol of her membership. Client reports that a species of wicked, subterranean hounds will rise, as they have done several times since 'The Beginning.' Client states that nobody believes their claims, as is the case with all things related to Bronxland."*

"Bronxland?" Omar looked skeptical. "Sounds like an amusement park."

Vaughn inspected the twisted images scrawled across Roselle's paperwork and shook his head, "Ain't nothing amusing about this."

They continued scanning the pages, when Kiki asked, "Did she say anything in here about how to kill them?"

Tom turned to Julie, "Yeah, she mentioned a truck, right? Something about deadly pies?"

Julie turned back to where the progress notes had been laid on the desk, but they were missing. She sifted through the piles of papers, confused.

"Anybody seen those progress notes?" Julie asked. "I swear I put them right here —"

GULP! Everyone turned to see Mo swallowing something down. As the lump of paper travelled down her throat, she wore a guilty look on her face.

"Sorry," Mo said to the group. "I thought we were done with it."

"What the hell, Mo!?" Omar was irate. "Julie got like a thousand pieces of paper in here and you gotta eat the only one we need?"

"The important ones taste better," Mo said. "I'd be happy to spit it back up... but I chewed the crap out of it"

The crew exchanged dejected looks.

"I'm sorry!" Mo yelled, getting emotional, "I couldn't help it!"

"It's okay, Mo," Julie said, comforting her with a hand on her back, "We'll figure something out."

Vaughn noticed that the wicks on the candles around the room were running low. He looked up at Tom, "We don't have all night."

Tom started wracking his brain. The beasts were scared of light, but the only light they had was fire, and the hallway was pissing from the sprinklers. Tom knew he'd have to get creative if he was going to make it to the Doctor's office with any limbs left. He scanned the room and spotted an umbrella being stored inside a wire mesh wastepaper basket. From there, his eyes shot to a straight-neck lamp on top of Julie's desk. The lamp had a long, study support pole extending from its base and a large lampshade fixed to the top.

"You got any duct tape?" Tom asked.

Julie looked skeptical, but seeing that Tom's wheels were turning, she reached into her desk drawer and tossed him a roll of duct tape.

Tom ripped the cord from the back of the desk lamp and threw it aside, then stacked the small trash can upright on top of the lamp's shade. Tom began duct taping the two items together while the others watched with curiosity. Next, he opened the umbrella and taped its long handle to the rim of the trash bin.

Finally, Tom ripped the tape, the three items successfully joined, then turned to Julie, "Got any papers we don't need?"

Intrigued, Julie nodded. She reached into a filing cabinet and handed over some old files. Tom began crumpling them up and tossing them into the basket.

"Oh, good thinking," Kiki said, finally seeing the vision for his creation. She moved closer and began helping Tom fill the trash bin with burnables.

"If I'm going out there, I need more than a candle," Tom said.

With the trash bin looking good and full, Tom grabbed the pole of the desk-lamp-turned-torch and moved it around the room to test its durability. He swung it side to side, and seeming satisfied with its strength, he stepped towards the office door.

Tom picked up a candle and was about to ignite his makeshift torch, when he paused and turned around to face the group. His hands were trembling.

"So," Tom said in a quavering voice, "Anybody coming with me?"

It was Tom's attempt at a joke, knowing full well that the

mission he was embarking on was likely suicidal, which is why he was utterly shocked when Vaughn stepped forward.

"I am."

A wave of hope rushed through Tom's body; he felt suddenly empowered and grateful that he'd been forgiven for his misdeeds, until Vaughn clarified:

"Only because I don't trust you."

Vaughn stretched his neck side to side, then swung his arms back and forth, getting loose for the upcoming battle.

He realized everyone was watching him, awaiting an explanation.

"Somebody's gotta make sure he don't bounce without us," Vaughn said.

Tom felt hurt by Vaughn's lack of faith, but it made perfect sense considering the picture Tom had painted of himself. In their eyes, he was a sad, privileged, self-serving liar covered in subterranean hound jizz. If the tables were turned, Tom wouldn't trust that sort of person with his life either.

"I'll go," Kiki said, as she stepped in front of Vaughn and motioned to the others. "They need you in here more than they need me."

Vaughn didn't like the idea.

Kiki turned to the others, "Right?"

Nobody wanted to respond, until Omar shrugged, "I mean, no offense to you, Kiki. If this were a dance competition, I'd want you on my team a hundred percent. But if we gotta punch monsters in the face, I'ma go with Vaughn."

Kiki gave Vaughn a look that read, *see?*

Vaughn shook his head, "I still don't like it."

"You don't have to," Kiki said. "You just have to think rationally. You know my situation. If anyone here is gonna take risks, it should be me."

Kiki locked eyes with Vaughn. Looking forlorn, Vaughn began to nod. His resignation indicated that there was something that Vaughn understood about Kiki that Tom didn't. Tom found the interaction quite strange.

Vaughn stepped aside for Kiki, and she joined Tom at the office door. Tom was hoping to catch a smile from Kiki, but it never came. *Oh yeah,* Tom thought, *flirting during a suicide mission is weird.* Nonetheless, Tom was relieved that Vaughn had been replaced by someone who didn't appear to hate his guts.

"So how will we know if you made it there okay?" Julie asked.

"Word," Omar said. "Y'all gotta let us know or else we'll just be sitting in here like bozos waiting for help that ain't coming."

Nobody had thought that far ahead.

Vaughn stepped towards the door's window and peered down the hall towards Doctor Ellison's office. Since Julie's office was located on the same side of the hallway as the Doctor's, his office door was out of view.

And then Vaughn was hit with an idea, "Ellison's flashlight. When y'all make it over there, shine it down the hall and flash it three times."

Tom and Kiki nodded at Vaughn.

There wasn't much else to say. The group exchanged tense looks, and a nervous energy filled the room.

Suddenly, Mo rushed forward and gave Kiki a bear hug.

"Promise me you won't die," Mo said.

Kiki chuckled and hugged Mo back, "That would be a bullshit promise, Mo. You know that."

With tears in her eyes, Mo looked up at Kiki, "Fine. Then promise me you'll try your hardest not to."

"I promise," Kiki said.

Mo retreated to Julie, who threw her arm around her.

"Good luck," Omar said, as he gave Kiki a fist bump. He turned to Tom, hesitated for a second, then extended his fist.

"Fix what you broke, homie," Omar told him. A look of determination on his face, Tom bumped Omar's fist, feeling encouraged by the small gesture.

Tom turned to look at Vaughn who, rather than blessing them with departing words, held out the open box of matches.

It was time.

Tom and Kiki each reached in to grab a match.

"What are you guys gonna do?" Tom asked Vaughn.

Vaughn shrugged, then smirked, "Wait for you to save the day."

Vaughn spun the match box in his hand, so that the striking surface faced out. With that, Tom struck the match and began igniting the papers inside his waste-bin-lamp-torch. Kiki struck hers, and joined in firing it up.

Tom and Kiki turned to the face door, and shared a quick look as they took one last deep breath. Finally, Tom popped open the umbrella above the flaming waste bin, and gave Kiki a nod.

Kiki opened the door, and the light from the torch sent the creatures scattering in the darkness. Tom held the torch above his head, making sure to emanate light in all directions. He stepped into the hissing, mist-filled hallway, with Kiki right behind him, and as soon as they crossed the threshold, Vaughn slammed and locked the door behind them.

Mo, Omar, and Julie ran up to the door's window to try and catch a glimpse of Tom and Kiki's mission.

"Everybody get ready," Vaughn said.

The others turned from the door to see Vaughn grabbing his meat cleaver.

"What are you talking about?" Julie asked.

Vaughn moved to the door's window to check in on the action, "He's got that stuff on him, so the creatures are gonna follow them towards Ellison's office." He spun around to face the crew, "The exit staircase is in the opposite direction."

They all sported reluctant looks.

"But... I thought the plan was to wait for them here," Omar said.

Vaughn shrugged, "Y'all can stay if you want, but I'm making a run for it." He turned back towards the door and added, "This might be our last chance."

8

TOUGH CALLS

om and Kiki crept down the hall under the light of their torch, which was so far surviving the sprinkler downpour thanks to Julie's trusty umbrella. As the flickering light shined down the hall in all directions, they could make out the limbs of beasts teetering along the edge of darkness, retreating from the light.

The hissing from the sprinklers reminded Tom of the white noise machine he would use to fall asleep when his mom and dad argued back home. He was grateful to have the sound now; the last thing he wanted to hear was a gang of monsters arguing over which one of them had dibs on devouring his heart.

And Kiki's.

Tom still couldn't figure out why she'd come along with him. Their backs were touching as they moved down the hall, and Tom was taken by how firm her body was. A thin, soaked hospital gown stuck to Kiki's wet skin, revealing her curvaceous body. She was freaking beautiful, Tom realized. He also realized that his brain was probably just trying to distract him from becoming overwhelmed by the terror of their situation. His friends at school would talk about how they'd rub one out whenever they felt stressed out about finals, or the SAT's, or after posting something on IG and anxiously waiting to get likes. It was a way to escape the stress. Tom wondered if he should tell Kiki that feeling her voluptuous body against his was helping him survive the invasion.

"Tom!" Kiki yelled.

Tom turned to find Kiki pointing up at the umbrella, the fabric of which was quickly melting from the flames.

Oh shit.

They shared a look and began racing down the hall, side by side, towards Doctor Ellison's office. They reached the door, and Kiki started pounding on it with her fist.

"Doctor Ellison, open up!" She screamed.

Tom looked up to see the hole in the umbrella growing larger, and water from the sprinklers was beginning to douse the fire. The flames were shrinking, and when Tom turned around to face the hallway, he could see figures in the darkness moving closer.

Tom whipped around and joined Kiki, who was still pounding on the door, "IT'S TOM WALTON. OPEN THE DOOR!"

The creatures shrieked, and they both spun around. With their backs against the door, Tom and Kiki helplessly watched the figures approach. The flames were now barely as luminous as a weak candle, and the monsters were close enough to smell. The scent of decaying meat was about to make Tom gag, when suddenly, the door behind them flew open —

Tom and Kiki fell backwards into the Doctor's office. Tom dropped the torch lamp, which shattered on the floor, but the creatures shrieked and scrambled away from the light emanating from the doctor's office. Tom and Kiki scrambled further into the office as the Doctor slammed the door shut.

Doctor Ellison locked the door and turned to Tom and Kiki. They were surprised to see him wearing a luxurious, white bath robe, with a cigar in one hand a glass of brown liquor in the other. A record player spun in the corner, filling the room with classical music.

"Thank you for coming," Doctor Ellison said. "I've been so painfully bored."

Tom and Kiki were too baffled to speak. They looked around and saw that the doctor had an LED-powered glowing orb stationed on a bookshelf, and a fancy tabletop fireplace burning on his desk. The calm, safe environment felt worlds away from the grim reality outside that door, Tom thought.

'Surprised to have you back, Kiki. You seemed a little...," Ellison searched for the right word, *"Defensive* after our last visit."

Tom looked over at Kiki and could see her trying to control her rage. Tom still didn't know what transpired between them, but he could sense that the doctor-patient relationship was not a healthy one.

Ellison smiled smugly, then asked, "Some scotch?"

Normally, Tom drank everything he could get his hands on. But he wasn't in the mood to drink. He couldn't articulate why, until Kiki did it for him.

"You do realize there are monsters outside this door trying to eat us, right?" Kiki said, the disgust in her voice loud and clear.

The Doctor shrugged, disturbingly calm. It reminded Tom of the way his father would respond to tough questions from the interviewers on the local NY news stations. Whether he was being asked to comment on pandemics, irreversible climate change, or police brutality, his father always kept it cool. Tom once asked his father why he seemed so unconcerned about these issues, and Senator Walton said that money bought immunity. As long as Tom didn't blow the family fortune on booze and bitcoin, his dad said, they would be safe for generations.

"So that's a no on the scotch? Suit yourself," the Doctor said, as he gulped down what was left in his glass. "I figured I'd might as well get comfortable. Called 9-1-1 over an hour ago, but you know the police response in a zip code like this... let's just say the Bronx is not exactly a top-priority borough."

Doctor Ellison walked over to his desk and grabbed his cell phone.

"But, that's why you're here, little Walton," he said, then tossed the phone over to Tom. "Call your father and get us out of here."

Tom held the phone in his hands and glanced over at Kiki. Something was on Tom's mind, but Kiki couldn't figure out what.

Tom looked up at the Doctor, "You didn't even ask about the others."

A light went off in Kiki's head — *the others!* Kiki jumped up, snatched the Doctor's flashlight off his desk, and hurried to the door's window. As per the game plan, she flashed the light on and off three times to signal to the rest of the crew that they'd made it safely.

"The others?" the Doctor asked, genuinely confused.

"The other patients, your own employees..." Tom said.

With frigid indifference, the doctor replied, "What about them?"

Tom shook his head in disbelief, "You don't seem to care whether they're dead or alive."

The Doctor chuckled, then poured himself another glass of scotch. He took a seat in his gaudy leather chair and reclined back.

"Son, I didn't bring you in here to teach me a lesson on morality," the Doctor said. "Survival of the fittest is nothing new, you know."

"Do *you* know?" Kiki asked, as she turned from the door. "For a doctor, your critical thinking skills are seriously lacking. The 'fittest' can be the most altruistic and loving. It's contextual. Darwin's theory doesn't imply selfishness and violence."

The Doctor looked at Kiki with an irritated smile, "Wow, you're *so* articulate."

Kiki sighed, disappointed, then turned to Tom, "Since they probably don't teach this in your school, I just want to point out that that right there is what's called a microaggression. The

Doctor's statement implied that it's unusual for people of my race to be intelligent."

Tom listened to Kiki intently. He replayed the interaction in his head and nodded, realizing that it truly was a shitty dig dressed in a compliment.

"I appreciate your perspective on Darwinian theory," the Doctor said, as he threw back a hefty gulp of scotch, then rose to his feet. Looking down at Kiki, he continued, "But I guess the fact of the matter is... I *choose* violence."

Doctor Ellison flashed a sinister smile at Kiki, then looked at Tom.

"Now call your father, before I get upset."

Vaughn peered through the window of Julie's office into the hallway.

"They're inside," he said, as he turned back to the group. "It's go time."

Omar and Mo looked torn, and both of them turned to Julie for guidance. Julie noticed that Vaughn was also staring back at her, seemingly asking her opinion on the matter, without actually asking.

"Remember when we talked about taking responsibility for our choices?" Julie asked. The group responded with nods, and Julie went on, "If we decide to leave now, and something happens to one of us, or something happens to Kiki and Tom, we need to be able to live with those outcomes."

They all took a second to think. Except for Vaughn.

"Those same things could happen if we stay in here," Vaughn said. "To me, it feels worse if we don't even try."

Omar nodded, "I'm with Vaughn. I'ma regret doing nothing. If we make it out alive, I can get my people to roll up with AKs and light them things up."

They turned to Mo.

"I would rather stay safe and wait it out here, but the truth is, we don't really know how the monsters work," Mo said.

"What do you mean?" Julie asked.

"They might be afraid of light, or they might just be adjusting to it because they've been living underground for god knows how long," Mo explained. "It might be like going to the kitchen in the middle of the night for a snack. At first, the light from the fridge is blinding, but then your eyes start to adjust... and then you can camp out and eat whatever you want."

Omar, Vaughn and Julie stared at Mo, eyes wide with fright, until Julie broke the silence.

"Let's get the hell out of here."

Tom dialed his father's number and hit the call button.

"Put it on speaker," Doctor Ellison said. The Doctor was towering over Tom, who was sitting in a comically small chair on the visiting side of the Doctor's desk. But Tom knew what that was all about, since his father employed the same power play in his own office; the Senator would make guests sit in short chairs in order to toy with their self-esteem and make them feel small in his presence. Tom couldn't help but notice how well the strategy was working. He felt tiny as he looked up at the Doctor lurking above him, swirling scotch around his glass, impatiently waiting for the call to connect.

Finally, the phone rang.

And rang.

And rang...

Tom hadn't even considered that his dad might not pick up. He was calling from a strange number, after all. Kiki, who was peeking out of the office door's window scanning for predators, turned to look back at Tom. Tom caught her glance and could see the worry on her face; they both knew they were screwed if his dad didn't pick up the phone.

Finally, a fourth ring gave way to a muffled grumble on the other end.

"Dad?" Tom asked, gripping the phone tight.

"For Christ's sake Tom," Senator Walton said, sounding irritated and sleepy. "What do you want?"

"Dad, I need your help! I'm trapped in the Bronx and we're being attacked by some kind of underground alien beasts or something —-"

"Woah woah, slow down," Senator Walton said. "Did you say you're in the *Bronx*? What the hell are you doing up there?"

Tom looked at Kiki, unsure how to answer. Now was not the time to explain to his father all the ways in which the Senator's twisted values, emotional immaturity, and god awful communication skills had most certainly contributed to Tom's jumping off a bridge.

Or maybe it was.

"I'm at Bronx Memorial," Tom said. He took a deep breath before going on, "I tried to kill myself."

The words just hung there. Kiki gave Tom a supportive nod, while Doctor Ellison rolled his eyes and stirred the air, motioning for Tom to hurry up and get to the point.

"God dammit, Thomas," Senator Walton said, exhaling a sigh of disappointment into the phone, "I told you to take it easy on the hard stuff."

Tom was outraged by his father's approach, "Dad, will you just listen to me!? I didn't call for you to chew me out, I called because I need your help!" Tom yelled, getting desperate.

"Okay, okay... is the media on this yet?" His father asked.

Tom looked baffled, "I have no idea... I don't think so."

"Good, that's good," Senator Walton said, relieved. "Then just hang tight. I'll send a car over and we'll get you fixed up."

Frustrated by his dad's nonchalance, Tom exploded, "You're not fucking hearing me! There are aliens in here trying to kill us!"

"Illegals?" Senator Walton asked, not at all joking. "Tell them that if they put their hands on you, your father will have their entire family deported.”

“No, I’m not talking about immigrants, I’m talking about —“

Suddenly, Doctor Ellison snatched the phone from Tom.

“Senator Walton,” Ellison spoke into the phone. “My name is Doctor Ellison, and I’m the medical director at Bronx Memorial Hospital.”

“Okay, and why am I speaking with you?” Senator Walton asked. “Put my son back on.”

Doctor Ellison smirked at Tom as he spoke, “Your son’s fine, I’m taking good care of him. But I want to make clear that the situation here is dire. Several people have already lost their lives in the attacks.”

“Lost their *lives*?” Senator Walton asked, sounding more awake now. “What kind of program are you running over there, doc? Get control of your hospital.”

“Oh, it’s under control where we are. I wanted to let you know that I’ve got your son in my office with me, and I’m personally keeping him safe.”

“I appreciate that, doc,” Senator Walton said. “Keep up the good work and help should be there soon.”

“I might,” Doctor Ellison said.

“I’m sorry?” Senator Walton asked.

“I might keep up the good work. If you make sure to clear my name with the Medical Board. You see, Senator Walton, I can’t transfer out of this hellhole while I’m still on probation for some minor... infractions. And I know you’re a well-connected man.”

Doctor Ellison winked at Tom. Tom and Kiki shook their heads in disgust.

“You got it, scumbag,” Senator Walton said, “Now put my son back on.”

Doctor Ellison looked both proud and offended by the abrupt interaction.

"Uh huh... thanks," Ellison said, before passing the phone back to Tom.

"Dad," Tom said. "Please hurry."

"Where in the hospital are you?"

"Fourth floor, in Four West. The psychiatric wing."

"Jesus," Senator Walton mumbled to himself. "Alright, hang in there. Help will be there soon. You're a smart kid, Tom. Trust yourself."

"Thanks dad," Tom said. "I will."

It was the nicest thing his dad had ever said to him.

"And be careful around that doctor," Senator Walton said. "A lotta those M.D.'s are sociopaths, and this one sounds like a true lowlife."

Tom looked up at Doctor Ellison, then replied, "You're on speakerphone, Dad."

"Good," Senator Walton said. "We aren't sharing any secrets. I'm sure that deep down inside, the doctor knows that his life had zero significance until the Waltons came into it."

Doctor Ellison smirked and sipped from his glass of scotch, coming to terms with the fresh feeling of having a bruised ego.

The room fell quiet. It was time to end the call. Tom figured it could be the last time he'd ever speak with his dad, so he decided to try something new.

"I love you Dad," Tom blurted out.

Tom could feel his face turning red, slightly embarrassed that he'd gone there, but he was hopeful that he might hear those comforting words mirrored back —

"Take care son."

Click.

VAUGHN PEERED OUT THE WINDOW, his hand on the knob, then turned to face Julie, Omar and Mo. Everybody looked nervous.

"Who's first?" Vaughn asked.

They glanced around at each other, then Omar raised his hand.

"I'm the slowest," Omar said. "I'll need the most time to get down those stairs."

The crew shared nods. It made sense.

Omar scanned the room and grabbed one of the flickering tea light candles off the top of a filing cabinet.

"No lights," Vaughn said. "If Mo's right, and they've gotten used to the light, it'll only help them see us."

Looking hesitant, Omar placed the candle back on the cabinet.

Mo raised her hand, "I'll go second. My legs are short."

Vaughn nodded, then looked at Julie.

"I run track," Vaughn told her. "So I'll go last."

"Are you sure?" Julie asked.

Vaughn nodded vehemently, then turned to Omar.

"You ready?" Vaughn asked.

Omar shrugged. *Not really.*

"Keep it slow until you get to the end of the hall, then run for your life," Vaughn said. He gave Omar a pat on the back, "You got this."

Omar slapped his belly and shook his head at Vaughn, "I shoulda been doing them workouts with you bro. We get outta here, you teaching me how to get ripped."

"No doubt," Vaughn said. He gave Omar a fist bump.

Vaughn quietly opened the door a crack. Omar poked his head out and peered down the hall, where the beasts were skulking around the outside of Ellison's office. The hissing sprinklers masked the sound of Omar's footsteps as he crept out into the hall. Omar stayed close to the wall, and began tip-toeing towards the rec room. When he checked back over shoulder to see if the creatures were onto him, he saw Vaughn leaning out the door to Julie's office, waving him to keep going.

Finally, Omar got to the end of the hall, and Vaughn watched him disappear around the corner.

Vaughn turned to the others inside the office.

"Mo, you're up," he said.

Mo crept past Vaughn and followed in Omar's footsteps. She moved like a cat, barely touching the floor as she swiftly moved down the hall. Vaughn watched her reach the end of the corridor, before dashing out of sight.

"Vaughn," Julie said, her voice full of concern.

Vaughn turned around to see Julie looking exceptionally anxious.

"What's up?" he asked.

Julie pointed to a floor to ceiling mirror that was leaned against the wall, and when Vaughn turned, he saw it right away. As the room dimmed in the dying candlelight, a glowing red substance was pulsating on the back of his hospital gown.

"I just noticed it. Must be from when you guys were back-to-back in the rec room," Julie said. "Some of it rubbed off on you."

Vaughn turned to inspect the goo on his shoulder, and pulled his hospital gown aside to see that it had soaked through to his skin. He tried to wipe it off to no avail. Vaughn was seething, but he knew that blaming the Walton kid now would get him nowhere.

"Just wanted to point it out," Julie said. "Make sure you run fast."

Vaughn shook his head, looking suddenly dejected.

"I can't go," Vaughn declared.

"What? Sure you can," Julie said, puzzled. "What did we say about believing in yourself —"

"It's not that," Vaughn cut in. "If I leave with this stuff on me, they're gonna follow me out... Last thing I wanna do is let these things loose in our community. There's enough monsters out there already."

Julie looked deep into Vaughn's eyes, and his determination

was clear. After years of working with people, Julie could tell when somebody's mind was made up. Sometimes it wasn't even worth arguing.

"So what are you going to do?" Julie asked.

Vaughn shrugged. He hadn't thought about it.

"Stay here and hope that you find some help," Vaughn said. He grabbed his meat cleaver and held it up, "Maybe kill me an alien or two."

Julie placed a hand on Vaughn's shoulder.

"If I ever decide to have children, which is highly unlikely considering my Bumble tragedies of late," Julie continued, "I hope they have a heart like yours. You're a good kid, Vaughn."

"Thanks," Vaughn said, his eyes cast down. "Can I ask you something?"

Julie nodded.

"What's my diagnosis?"

"What do you *think* your diagnosis is?"

"I don't know... I was reading through that book with all the disorders, thought maybe I had Conduct Disorder or Oppositional Defiant Disorder?"

Julie looked amused, then began shaking her head.

"There's nothing wrong with you, Vaughn."

Vaughn looked thrown by the response.

"Stop playing with me. Even *I* know my anger ain't normal..."

"Anger is a secondary emotion," Julie said. "That means we use it to cover up more vulnerable feelings like pain and fear. And when you grow up in a culture that shames people, especially young men, for expressing those emotions, what choice do you have? You are a human being responding to your environment."

Vaughn stared at Julie, processing her words.

Julie continued, "But you have to keep in mind that although your anger makes sense, it doesn't mean that it's serving you. The Buddha says that holding onto anger is like drinking poison and expecting the other person to die."

Vaughn gave his mind a second to digest.

"So I need to let go of my anger?" he asked.

Julie nodded, "You're going to need to experience what's underneath that anger to free yourself internally. But you might want to save that work for *after* you chop off some alien heads."

The comment caught Vaughn by surprise. When he noticed Julie's growing smirk, he chuckled appreciatively. Vaughn wanted to express to Julie how much she'd helped him in his short time at Bronx Memorial, but he figured she knew, since she healed people for a living. Instead, Vaughn offered Julie a fist bump with his free hand, then reached for the doorknob.

He paused and turned back to Julie, "Do me a favor?"

Julie's eyebrows said *sure*.

"Promise me you'll make it out alive," Vaughn said. "Nobody's gonna believe a bunch of crazy Bronx kids about what happened here tonight."

Julie clenched her jaw to fight back tears. It was so true, and so sad.

"As long as you promise me something," Julie said. "Remember that anybody who calls you crazy is dangerous. They're the ones who have fallen in line and are perfectly happy with the way things are."

"So stay wild?" Vaughn asked.

Julie smiled, "Exactly."

"I can do that," Vaughn said, grinning.

With that, he twisted the knob, slowly pushed the door open, and Julie crept out into the hall. He watched her slide safely down the corridor, until finally, she disappeared.

Vaughn closed and locked the door, then turned around to lean against it when a horrific shriek echoed through the hallways. Vaughn took a moment to soak in the grim reality of his situation, then slid down to the floor, hopeless and full of dread, and buried his face in his hands.

. . .

Doctor Ellison snatched the phone away from Tom and tossed it onto his desk. Kiki saw the phone land right next to a loaded syringe of booty juice.

"Your father's something, huh?" Doctor Ellison asked Tom.

Tom didn't know what to say.

"It's funny, you affluent kids are just as screwed up as the poor ones," Doctor Ellison looked at Kiki, "No offense."

Both Tom and Kiki flipped Ellison the bird. Ellison smiled and began browsing through his collection of vinyl records as he went on, "Substance abuse, depression, anxiety, high rates of envy amongst peers, a sense of self-worth derived entirely from achievement, all kinds of chauvinism and narcissism, a low capacity for tenderness, the inability to form deep social connections…" The Doctor found a vinyl he liked, and pulled it from the sleeve as he turned to Tom.

"Any of that sound familiar?"

"No," Tom said.

The Doctor chucked, "Of course not." He adjusted the needle on his record player.

Of course, everything the Doctor had said was spot on, but Tom didn't want to give him the satisfaction. He also didn't want Kiki thinking he was a chauvinist. He didn't know what the word meant, but it sounded like the word socialist, and his dad always called his mom that name whenever they argued about money. Tom didn't know what that word meant either, and neither did his dad, according to his mom.

A classical violin piece began playing through two mahogany tower speakers, as Doctor Ellison turned to face Tom.

"All of these struggles, however, can be avoided with the right parents. Parents who are warm, sensitive, and responsive act as protective factors so that kids like you don't turn into spoiled little tyrants. My parents weren't perfect, but they weren't as bad as your father. It makes perfect sense that you wanted to kill yourself."

"What's your point, asshole?" Kiki asked.

Doctor Ellison smirked, seemingly aroused by the animosity in the room. He sat back down at his desk and swirled his glass of scotch.

"My point is that even when we make it out of here, the Walton boy's prognosis isn't good. Chances are, he's probably still going to kill himself one of these days. Right Tom?"

Tom was confused. He hadn't thought about killing himself for several hours now; it was the longest he'd gone in years. But suddenly, he felt his thoughts spiraling towards a familiar sense of hopelessness when —

BOOM!

Something shattered through the glass of the door's window. They all spun around to see that a limb covered in wiry, black hair had punched through the window and was quickly retreating back into the hall, a set of razor sharp claws leaving deep depressions in the metal door. Kiki and Tom jumped up and scrambled away from the door, joining the doctor behind his desk.

The Doctor's smug expression was gone. He sat up in his chair and placed his glass of scotch on the desk.

"They're getting more brazen," Ellison said.

He reached down, opened a desk drawer, and pulled out an antique pistol with intricate wood carvings and silver engravings.

"I didn't want to have to use this, since it brings down the value," the Doctor said, as he calmly loaded bullets. "This pistol once belonged to Andrew Jackson's next door neighbor," he proudly proclaimed.

"My dad's got one that belonged to Andrew Jackson himself," Tom said, matter of factly. He didn't mean anything by it, but the Doctor looked irate. The sudden outrage on the Doctor's face made Kiki laugh.

The Doctor mimicked Tom's voice by raising it several octaves, *"My dad's got one that belonged to Andrew Jackson himself."*

He cocked the gun and pointed it at Tom, who immediately raised his hands.

"Woah, I'm sorry!" Tom was more confused than he was scared.

"Ha! Talk about envy amongst peers," Kiki said.

The Doctor shot a look at Kiki that told her to be careful, when...

BOOM! A huge dent formed in the center of the door. The Doctor whipped around and pointed the pistol towards the entrance. They could all see the monsters moving past the door's now broken window. Kiki grabbed the flashlight off Ellison's desk and shined it towards the opening.

"We have to keep the light on them," Kiki said.

Tom threw on his thinking cap, and quickly grabbed the Doctor's LED globe from the bookshelf and stepped closer to the door. He held it up high, making the entryway brighter than broad daylight. Satisfied, he turned to face Kiki and the Doctor, "If we keep it lit over here, we should be safe until help comes."

BOOM! A beast smashed into the door, and it sent Tom diving to the floor. He dropped the LED globe, which smashed to pieces and went dark. Tom turned around to see another monstrous claw bending the steel door from the window frame, despite Kiki directly exposing it with the Doctor's flashlight beam. The beasts were unrelenting, and cracks began forming along the walls surrounding the door frame.

Tom looked back at Kiki, spooked.

"They aren't scared of light anymore!" Kiki yelled.

POP! The Doctor fired a bullet that sent the beast reeling! The monster recoiled back into the hallway and screeched with pain. Tom rushed back behind the Doctor's desk and took cover, as Ellison quickly reloaded his smoking single shooter with another bullet.

With the core light source in the room gone, Kiki noticed that the red substance on Tom was glowing even more brightly.

"We need to get that stuff off of you somehow," she said, then turned to Ellison, "You have any of that medical grade soap in here?"

Doctor Ellison noticed the strange glowing substance on Tom's clothing and skin. He paused from reloading his gun.

"What is that?" he asked.

"I don't know," Tom said. "But I fell into it in the river. And I think the monsters are attracted to it."

The Doctor scoffed, then popped the bullet into his gun and cocked it.

"You know...," he began, his tone and demeanor becoming noticeably more vile, "Those creatures were leaving me alone with my eighteen year Macallan until you came waltzing in here wearing alien pheromones."

The Doctor stepped towards Tom.

Kiki, who was standing behind the Doctor, could tell that things were about to go south. She swiftly reached onto Ellison's desk, grabbed the syringe of booty juice, and concealed it behind her wrist.

BANG! The beasts were knocking. By now, they all knew the door hinges were only strong enough to survive three or four of those blows.

The Doctor raised his gun and pointed it at Tom.

"Get out," he said.

Tom gulped, "What do you mean?"

"Get out of my office," he said, cocking the gun. "*Now.*"

"But... those things," Tom glanced at the door, his voice trembling. "They're going to kill me."

"Yeah, what's wrong with you?!" Kiki yelled. "You can't just kill a kid!"

The Doctor didn't even turn to look at Kiki. He kept the gun trained on Tom and poked him in the chest with the barrel, urging him towards the door. "This kid might've just killed me by coming in here," Ellison said. "So I have no sympathy."

Kiki followed closely behind them, clutching the syringe tightly in her right hand. Finally, Tom reached the door.

"Please don't do this," Tom begged.

Kiki slowly turned the syringe around in her hand, needle out. She made eye contact with Tom, who noticed the syringe.

"Don't blame me, blame Darwin," Ellison said, as he motioned to the doorknob with his gun. "Some individuals must die to ensure the survival of the group. So, dearest Kiki and I thank you for your service."

Suddenly, Kiki lunged at the Doctor from behind and plunged the syringe deep into his backside —

"No, thank YOU!" She yelled.

The Doctor howled and pulled up, and as he swung around to attack Kiki, Tom grabbed hold of the pistol. Tom immediately remembered how strong Doctor Ellison was, as his body was flung around like a child being swung in circles during playtime. But Tom wouldn't let go of the gun. The Doctor cursed them both, when Kiki kicked Ellison hard between the legs. Ellison doubled over and fell to the floor, and Tom wrestled the gun free. Tom began scrambling away, when Ellison grabbed him by the ankle. Holding the gun by the barrel, Tom spun around, swung the butt at Doctor Ellison's face and clocked him in the side of the head. Ellison dropped to the floor, face first.

Tom looked at Kiki. *Holy shit.*

BOOM! A giant crack in the wall was growing larger, spidering towards the ceiling. They were running out of time.

Tom and Kiki scanned the room for escape routes that they could have somehow missed.

Kiki pointed to the window, "We need to break that."

"Why? If we jump from four stories up, we're dead," Tom said.

But Kiki was already on her feet. She picked up one of the doctor's wooden chairs, lifted it over her head, and smashed it against the glass. It cracked. She cocked back and swung it again. It cracked some more. She turned back to Tom.

"You gonna help me or what?" She screamed.

Tom jumped up and grabbed a chair. Unsure of exactly what he was doing, he lifted it over his head and bashed it into the window. Chunks of glass fell to the floor as a corner of the chair managed to break through.

"Watch out!" Kiki yelled. "I got this!"

Tom pulled his chair from the window, when Kiki cocked back and swung with all her might. The chair busted straight through and shards of glass came raining down on them. They covered their heads and ducked away, when suddenly, Kiki was grabbed from behind.

"You're a crafty one," Doctor Ellison said, his words slurred. "Too bad that dose can't take down a grown man. Only little gutter rats like you."

Tom turned to see Ellison holding Kiki in a chokehold, and he instinctually lifted the pistol to point it at the doctor.

Doctor Ellison laughed, "That gun's not for sharpshooting, kid. You'll put more holes in her than you will me."

"Just let her go," Tom said.

"I will," Ellison said. "If you jump out that window right now."

Tom glanced out the window. There was nothing but darkness.

"Or, I can snap her neck," Ellison said, as he choked Kiki harder. Tom wished he could consult Kiki about this. Did she *want* to be alive for an extra ten minutes? At this point, dying was inevitable. A snapped neck almost seemed like the easy way out of what was destined to be a gruesome end. But Kiki could barely breathe, let alone speak.

Tom assessed the situation. The whole reason he was at the hospital to begin with was because he'd failed to kill himself. The way Tom looked at it, he should be dead already. And since he'd made a death jump once before, it wasn't all that scary.

"Fine," Tom said, lowering the gun. "But let her go first. She can't breathe."

The Doctor grinned, "I'm the one with the power, little Walton. You don't call the shots." Kiki gasped for air, slapping at the Doctor's arms which were still wrapped around her neck like a vice.

"Now jump," Ellison said.

Tom looked at Ellison with hatred, but his concern for Kiki was forcing him to act. Resigned, he stepped backwards towards the window, when —

BOOM! Tom turned to see a beast plow through the door and pounce on the Doctor's back. Tom couldn't tell the difference between the monster's shrieks and the Doctor's screams, when he spotted Kiki crawling out from underneath the pile. As she rushed toward Tom, Tom looked over Kiki's shoulder and saw the other two beasts squeezing through the doorway.

When Tom glanced back at Kiki, he was shocked to see her approaching him at full speed. Without warning, she barreled into Tom's chest and tackled him backwards, and before Tom could even think, they both went sailing out of the fourth story window.

They fell through the air, joined by a kaleidoscope of glass shards that shimmered from the moonlight above. It all seemed to happen in slow motion for Tom, who found the moment strikingly beautiful. This was *so* much more interesting than suicide, Tom thought. Still in the clutches of Kiki's arms, he gently closed his eyes.

And they made impact.

9

THE GREATEST TEACHER

Vaughn peeked through the window of Julie's office, trying to catch a glimpse of the action down the hall. The sounds of gunshots, human screams, alien war cries, concrete demolition, and shattering glass made it abundantly clear that shit was going down. But with the lights off in Doctor Ellison's office, Vaughn couldn't see a thing.

Think, Vaughn. Think.

Vaughn turned away from the door and paced towards the opposite wall's floor to ceiling window. Not a bad view, Vaughn thought. It looked out across the street, where nearby rooftops were covered in generators, air vents, and sloppy practice graffiti. Vaughn peered down at the street below, where a row of flickering street lights painted the asphalt a familiar tint of orange. Street lights usually gave Vaughn a warm feeling inside, but right now they looked like burning flames. Funny how quickly your world can come to resemble hell, he thought.

There was no sign of Julie, Omar and Mo, but Vaughn knew that if they made it down the stairs, the nearest exit was on the other side of the building. Vaughn scanned the block, all way up to the Chevron station on the corner, which was lit up like a film shoot. He never understood why a business that charged a fortune for a gallon of energy wasted so much power on making three AM feel like broad daylight. And then he noticed something he hadn't seen earlier:

A small box truck painted haphazardly in orange, white, and blue paint was parked next to the gas station's free air pump. Vaughn wouldn't have thought much of it, except that those were the colors of the New York Mets, and this was clearly Yankee territory. On top of the bizarre colors, Vaughn saw a giant black 'X' painted on the roof of the truck.

Curious, Vaughn hurried back to Julie's desk, where papers from Roselle's folder were scattered about. Vaughn began re-inspecting, searching for whatever it was that made the image he'd just seen ring some kind of bell. Finally, he came across pages of drawings and scribbles that Roselle must have completed during arts and crafts time, and froze.

All of the drawings were done in crayons of two colors: *blue and orange.*

Vaughn held up one of the pages horizontally. It was a tricolor flag that he recognized, but couldn't place. The top band was orange, the middle was white, and the bottom band was blue. There was a wreath in the center of the white band, which encircled a golden Eagle and a coat of arms that featured a banner with three words on it:

"Ne Cede Malis."

Vaughn knew it was Latin, but he had no clue what it meant. He flipped the piece of paper around, and on the back, Roselle had written, *"BRONXLAND,"* with the *'X'* in emphasized in bold. That's when Vaughn recognized it as the Bronx borough flag, which he saw every day as he passed the 161st Street courthouse on his way to school. Still, he couldn't understand why Roselle was calling it "Bronxland" and not "The Bronx." Underneath that, she wrote the words, *"Do Not Yield to Evil."* Vaughn was hoping it might be a translation of the Latin words, but he doubted an official borough flag would include the word "evil." Or maybe there was a whole lot about his hometown that he didn't know.

Vaughn thought back to the police report that Julie had read aloud earlier, specifically the part about Roselle telling the police her truck was *"full of deadly pies."* And suddenly, it hit him. Vaughn remembered from his nefarious internet research that PIES was an acronym that stood for: Power supply, Initiator, Explosive, and Switch. They were the main components of an IED. Vaughn knew at that moment that the colorful box truck across the street didn't belong to some die hard Mets fan with a flat tire.

It was Roselle's truck.

And it was full of explosives.

CONCRETE IS SOFTER than it looks, Tom thought.

He was lying on his back, looking up at the sky when time stood still. But as glass and debris continued to fall around him, he realized that he was the only thing frozen in space.

"In here!" Kiki yelled.

Tom was happy to realize that he had a friend with him in the afterlife. But since he was most definitely on his way to hell, he wondered why Kiki was along for the ride, then figured her flight to heaven must have gotten rerouted.

Tom felt something digging into his back, so he reached around and touched the fibrous knot of a rope beneath him. Tom rolled over, and through the holes of a thick safety net, he stared at the paved sidewalk two stories below. Tom appraised his surroundings, and saw that the net was attached to some rusted scaffolding. When he looked back up towards the window he'd fallen from, he could see that the scaffolding extended all the way to the rooftop. This was the first time he'd seen the exterior of

Bronx Memorial, and it looked even crummier than he'd imagined.

But the good news was that he wasn't dead; he'd landed in a hammock made for fallen debris. Tom took a second to recognize the significance of that last thought. Living felt like *good* news.

"Come on!" Kiki screamed.

Tom looked over to find Kiki inside the building, waving him towards a small, open window. A chorus of shrieks from above reminded Tom that the downside to surviving was that he still had to escape those vicious things. Tom scrambled across the netting and squeezed back inside through the little window, and Kiki slammed it shut behind him.

The first thing Tom noticed was that the floors were dry. There were no sprinklers on down here. On top of that, it was totally silent.

"Follow me," Kiki said, as she took off running down the hall. Tom chased after her into the darkness, using the sound of her footsteps to guide the way. He heard Kiki's pace slow, and when she turned into a nearby room, Tom followed her inside.

Remnants of streetlights shined through the room's sole window, illuminating the space with a warm, orange glow. Tom was immediately surprised to find what looked like a fully decorated bedroom. Kiki began rummaging through drawers and moving about the room like she'd been there before. And then Tom noticed a couple of picture frames on top of a dresser.

Tom stepped closer, and saw that one was a photo of Kiki dressed in a leotard, posing gracefully as a dancer for the camera. Another showed Kiki smiling with two girlfriends. An attractive bunch, for sure. Tom normally would have suggested that his friends meet her friends so they could be friends on the weekends, but right now he was more intrigued to find out why Kiki's room wasn't in Four West.

Finally, Kiki grabbed an iPhone from her nightstand drawer.

"I got it!" She said, as she held up her phone. She flipped it around to show a key hospital card, similar to the one that Julie had given Tom, fixed to the back of her iPhone case. Kiki appeared hopeful.

But Tom just looked at her, confused.

"I don't understand," he said. "What floor are we on?"

Kiki glanced at Tom, and she could see that he was onto her.

"The second," she said, just as the sounds of shattering glass echoed through the halls.

"We need to go, now!" Kiki snatched a photo that was tacked to a cork board on the wall, tucked it into her bra, then blew past Tom and out into the corridor. Tom took one last look at Kiki's room before rushing after her.

When Tom stepped out into the hallway, he peeked back at the window through which they entered, and could see the beasts trying to squeeze through the window frame. They appeared to be smashing the walls around the frame. Here we go again, Tom thought. He turned and bolted after Kiki.

Tom followed Kiki to the end of the hall, which opened into a large room, the layout practically identical to Four West. Kiki crossed the room to a set of double doors and held out her iPhone to the key sensor. The doors unlocked, and Kiki pushed through, bringing her into the entrance corridor. With Tom right behind her, she bolted towards the staircase door, and was about to yank it open when —

BOOM! A beast slammed against the door from inside the staircase. Kiki screamed and jumped back, crashing into Tom and sending them both to the floor. They sprung to their feet and began scrambling back through the double doors, but not before something caught Tom's eye.

Tom paused as he saw a sign on the wall that read:

"Two West - Oncology"

Oncology? Tom knew that word. He used to visit his grandpa in the oncology unit before he died, but he was a lot older than Kiki...

BOOM! The beast smashed against the staircase door again, and Tom knew the drill. He turned off his thoughts and sprinted after Kiki back into the main room. Kiki ran to the far side, where there a solid roll-down gate was bolted to a countertop, beneath a sign that read "*Pharmacy.*" Kiki moved to a side door, presented her key card, and the door unlocked. They scurried inside, then Kiki slammed it closed.

It was pitch black.

All they could hear were each other's breaths.

"Damn, was hoping we could make it down the stairs," Kiki said. "But I guess if we're gonna hide out anywhere, this is the spot."

Finally, Kiki turned on her iPhone's flashlight.

"Pharmacies around here are like Fort Knox." Kiki flashed her light towards the metal grate, "Pretty sure that gate right there is bulletproof."

Tom wasn't looking at the gate. He was staring at Kiki, trying to figure out which question to ask first. Start small, Tom thought.

"So you *knew* there was a safety net out there?" Tom asked.

"Correct. I wasn't trying to kill you," Kiki chuckled. "As you know, they're giving this building an expensive makeover, starting with the roof, so I've been watching coffee cups and beer cans fall onto that net for weeks."

Forget the soft questioning, Tom thought. This is an alien invasion.

"Why do you have a room in the cancer unit?" Tom asked.

"Hm, how do I best answer that?" Kiki feigned pensiveness, then smiled, "The medical marijuana down here is dank?"

She hoped for a laugh, but saw that Tom looked worried. Sad, even.

"Hey, you can't be more miserable than I am," Kiki told him.

"It's a rule on this floor... or at least it used to be, back before they started shutting things down here."

The room fell quiet, as Tom pondered the implications of it all. Finally, Tom interrupted the silence.

"I think it's your turn," he said.

Kiki look confused, so Tom clarified, "I've heard everyone's story except yours."

"You sure you wanna hear it?" Kiki asked. "It bums people out."

Tom took a seat on the counter, facing Kiki.

Yes.

With a reluctant smile, Kiki ambled over and sat down next to him. She took a deep breath, cleared her throat, then began:

"There's not much to it. I grew up a normal kid, had dreams, always wanted to be a dancer. Got into LaGuardia High School for dance, actually. Hate to brag, but I was really, really good... Sophomore year, stuff started going wrong. My family's house was right next to the chemical plant over in Hunts Point. We didn't think anything of it, until my grandma died of cancer, then my dad, then my mom, then my little sister... I had to move in with my cousin because I had nobody left. And then I got sick."

Kiki reached into her bra and pulled out the folded up photo she'd grabbed from her room. She passed it over to Tom, along with her phone, so that Tom could illuminate the image. The photo showed a much younger Kiki with a group of people that Tom assumed was her family, all of them smiling underneath a sky full of majestic fireworks.

"That was the last time we were all together," Kiki said. "The Macy's firework show, like five years back..."

"So that was on the Hudson River that year?" Tom asked.

"Yeah, I think so. How'd you know that?"

"They alternate between the east side and the west side each year. Our apartment was on the east side," Tom paused, before going on, "When I was a little kid, my mom and I would go up on the roof with a couple of fish nets to see if we could catch a fire-work or two."

Tom chuckled fondly at he memory. It made Kiki smile.

"I love that. Aren't fireworks the best? It's one of the few times people in this city truly come together. A million awestruck people, looking up at the sky, taking a moment to recognize that they're part of something bigger, something magical... It's beautiful."

Tom had never thought of the Macy's fireworks that way. To him, the show was nothing more than a decades-old marketing campaign that utilized colorful explosives. Nonetheless, Tom found himself nodding along with Kiki. He was beginning to realize that his tendency towards negativity and cynicism was a choice. Kiki was living, breathing proof there was a way of looking at the world that was full of wonder and curiosity. Tom wanted to spend more time around people like Kiki.

"I try not to think about the future much these days, but I was really hoping I'd live to see one more firework show. Unfortu-nately, these aliens seem hellbent on making sure that doesn't happen."

A crestfallen look washed over Tom's face.

"One more... so it's terminal?"

Kiki nodded, then slowly lifted her shirt up to expose her mid-section; it was covered in gnarly surgical scars from front to back.

"Started here with my bladder, then my kidneys, then my lungs, then my liver," Kiki said, tracing the multitude of deep indents in her skin.

Tom was listening, but not really. He was stuck in problem-solving mode, already thinking of the cutting edge treatments Kiki needed to explore, the way his grandfather did. He was about to begin making suggestions, when Kiki continued.

"But surgery's not cheap. Finally, my cousin's family couldn't

afford it anymore. Even if they could, my body couldn't take it...
And here I am."

"What about chemo? I mean, there are so many
treatments—"

Kiki reached up and grabbed her braids, then slowly pulled
them off her head. Tom was shocked to see her removing a wig,
which revealed a mostly bald head with thin hairs no longer than
an inch.

"I did chemo. Lots of it. Makes you feel awful. And it's not
how I want to spend my last few months."

Tom was speechless. He couldn't stop staring at Kiki's head.

"*Hot*, right?" Kiki asked with a sarcastic smile.

Tom didn't know how to answer that. It was shocking, that's
for sure. He felt like he'd been kicked in the stomach, but the more
Tom looked at Kiki, the more he realized that she was absolutely
perfect.

"You're beautiful," Tom said.

Oh shit, Tom thought. *I didn't mean to say that out loud.*

Kiki chuckled and shook her head.

"Why thank you, Tom Walton," Kiki said. "But before you
start thinking this is going to be like the romantic part of every
action film ever, where the guy and the girl make out, it ain't
happening."

Tom was thankful it was dark, because he felt his face turning
beat red.

"Oh, that's not at all where my head was at..." Tom said, lying.

"Good, because I've already been creeped out once today,"
Kiki said.

Tom knew right away what she was referencing.

"Doctor Ellison?" He asked.

Kiki nodded, then shook her head in disgust.

"I wanted to ask you what happened," Tom said, "But —-"

"It wasn't that serious," Kiki interjected. "The Doctor told me
he'd try to get me into this exclusive alternative cancer treatment

study, and said he'd let me know today if I was accepted. So I'm his office, and this pervert starts talking about how he wants something from me in return. I'm looking at him like, 'are you serious right now?' Obviously he was, because he reached out and touched my wig, so I slapped the shit out of him."

"You *slapped* him?"

"Hell yeah, Will Smith times ten," Kiki said, nodding with pride. "That's when you guys came to the door."

"But... what about the study?" Tom asked. "Did you get accepted?"

Kiki shrugged, "No idea. All I know is that there's not a study in the world that's worth letting that slimy man put his hands on me. Dying is hard enough. Dying knowing I wasn't true to myself, that's a whole different kind of brutal."

Tom wondered what being true to himself even looked like.

"Also, just to clarify," Kiki said. "The reason we aren't making out isn't because you're not cute. Or because you're the white devil. It's because I know it's not a good idea to get involved with someone right before they're about to leave town."

Tom had so much to say, but that last part confused him.

"Who's leaving town?" he asked.

"Me. I'm dying, remember?"

Oh yeah. Tom nodded, then cut short the awkward moment

—

"Can I ask you something?"

Kiki shrugged, *sure.*

"How come you seem so alive?"

"What do you mean?" Kiki asked.

"From the moment I got here, you've been dancing, joking, smiling," Tom said, looking confused. "And that's despite the fact that you're sick..."

Kiki sat down on the counter next to Tom.

"A popular belief in the cancer community is that death is the greatest teacher. It puts everything into perspective. Life is too short *not* to dance, you know. But most people don't realize it until it's too late... I remember back when my mom was sick, she asked me to make sure we played our favorite song before we took her off the ventilator... 'Dancing Queen' by ABBA. We loved that track, and it *always* made her dance. But by the time she reached the end, I put the song on for her, and she couldn't move a muscle. Saddest moment of my life," Kiki sniffled and shook her head, "I refuse to go out that way. I want to dance until the very end."

Tom was still trying to connect the dots.

"I still don't get it," Tom said. "Why were you in Four West?"

Kiki smiled, "I met Julie in the elevator one day, and asked her if I could spend some time up there. I heard it was full of kids who got tripped up, and for whatever reason, had forgotten what a gift it is to be alive. I admit, it's easy to lose hope when you live around here... but like I said, death is a bomb-ass teacher."

Kiki cleared her throat.

"I'll never understand the kind of suffering and pain someone like you must be going through to want to take your own life... But I do know the suffering and pain of somebody who wishes they could live, when that's just not an option."

The statement punched Tom in the gut. He continued to look at Kiki, who wore a somber expression, as he mulled over her words.

"Crazy... I guess now I've got both of those experiences," Tom said.

Kiki seemed confused, so Tom motioned to the hallway with a nod and clarified, "Killer aliens."

"Oh, right... So you're saying that you wish you could live now?" Kiki asked, filling with excitement.

Tom shrugged, a little bashful, though he didn't know why. It was as if the feeling of hope was so unfamiliar to his system that his body didn't know how to respond.

"Dude, I would've been the best therapist," Kiki said, chuckling.

"I disagree," Tom responded. Kiki appeared to be offended, until Tom quickly followed up with, "You already are."

Kiki looked flattered, "You're smooth, Tom. We're not gonna make out, but you're smooth."

"I'm not trying to make out with you!" Tom yelled, playfully. "But you do kinda make me feel like I exist. I think you're the first girl I've even looked in the eye since..." Tom trailed off, and Kiki noticed a shift in his demeanor.

"Your mom?" Kiki proposed.

Tom nodded. He sat quietly as he recalled the memories, "The worst part was, I never even got to apologize."

Kiki could feel Tom's pain. They sat in silence for a moment, until Kiki spoke up, "Since I'm kinda like a guru when it comes to death and grief, do you want to hear my advice?"

"Please," Tom said.

Kiki locked eyes with Tom.

"Say sorry in the way you behave."

Tom took that in. He couldn't see how it would eliminate his guilt, since he doubted his mom was somewhere up in the sky looking down on this actions. But maybe he didn't need to believe in the afterlife. According to biology, he did inherit about half his DNA from his mother. Tom was never the spiritual type, but this revelation felt profound. Maybe his mom was with him all the time. Not maybe. She *was* with him all the time. She was in his genes. She was a part of every cell in his body. It was science.

Kiki reached out and gently squeezed Tom's hand. Tom looked to Kiki, and peered deep into her eyes.

Tearful, he smiled, "You really should stick around for a while." Tom chuckled as tears fell down his cheeks. He wiped them away with his sleeve, and added, "The world needs more people like you."

Kiki caressed Tom's back in a nurturing gesture, when all of a sudden —

BANG! Something pierced through the pulldown gate.

Tom jumped from the countertop, and spun around to inspect the source of the sound. Oddly, he noticed that Kiki hadn't moved, and what he saw next made his stomach drop:

A bloodied alien claw was protruding through the center of Kiki's chest.

10

PAIN KILLERS

Vaughn needed to get to that truck.

He paced around Julie's office, rattling his brain for ideas. He needed protection, a way out. A meat cleaver was better than nothing, but it was definitely not enough to fend off a trio of aliens. Vaughn began searching Julie's office for anything he could use. He opened her desk drawer, hoping she'd have a pistol in the top drawer like everyone does in the movies, but she only had staplers, pencils, a box of latex gloves and a pile of COVID surgical masks. Vaughn was about to shut the drawer, then paused to pick up one of the masks.

COVID...

Vaughn's mind began to race. He hurried over to Julie's metal storage closet, and opened it up to find coats, shirts, and bags hanging from a rod. Vaughn was looking for something specific; he remembered seeing them all over TV when the pandemic was in full swing. Vaughn rifled through the items until finally, buried deep inside the closet, he spotted two white hazmat suits with a pair of gas masks hanging from each one.

He wasn't sure if it would work, but since he couldn't get that red stuff off of him, he figured he might be able to cover it up instead. If those suits could keep viruses out, he reasoned, they had to be able to keep the scent of alien eggs — or whatever the hell it was — in.

Vaughn hurried back to Julie's desk, grabbed a pair of nitrile surgical gloves, and threw them on. He carefully removed his glowing, wet hospital gown, balled it up, and placed it on the desk. In nothing but briefs, Vaughn returned to the closet, unzipped the hazmat suit and stepped into it. He pulled it up around his waist and put his arms inside, careful not to touch the outside of the suit, then zipped it up to his neck. He grabbed the gas mask off the hanger, put it over his face, then lifted the hood over his head and pulled the string tight to secure it around his mask.

Vaughn was now odorless. To the aliens, he was undetectable. At least that's what he needed to believe in order to go through with this. Vaughn knew his plan was not even half-baked, but he was running out of ideas.

The strategy was to open the door to Julie's office, toss the bait, and run.

If he managed to get outside, he could see about Roselle's truck, and try to figure out how to destroy the aliens once and for all.

But one step at a time.

Vaughn turned back to his pulsating hospital gown and, using papers from Roselle's file, he picked it up. He made sure not to make direct contact with the substance, then grabbed the meat cleaver with his free hand. Vaughn stepped to the door, peered through the small window, and saw nothing but darkness.

Vaughn unlocked the door, then paused to say a quick prayer.

God, please don't let them be hiding right outside this door.

Amen.

He took a deep breathe and swung the door open.

But there were no monsters. Just darkness and the sounds of water leaking from the now dribbling sprinklers.

Vaughn peeked his head out, checked both directions like he

was about to step out onto a dangerous highway, and saw nothing.

Using the balled up gown as bait, Vaughn stepped out into the corridor and flung the pulsating gown twenty feet down the hall towards the Doctor's office. He crumpled up the papers he used to grab hold of the gown, and flung those as well. Vaughn figured if the beasts followed the scent down that way, it would buy him more time to bolt the other way down the stairs.

But just as Vaughn was about to turn and book it, he looked at Ellison's office, and noticed there were faint lights twinkling in the distance. It took a second for him to realize he was looking at the skyline of Manhattan, through a gaping hole in the side of the building that cut straight through Ellison's office.

Kiki. The Walton kid. Doctor Ellison. They were all gone.

Damn, Vaughn thought. Kiki didn't deserve to die like that. But Vaughn also knew that she was terminally ill, and so he took solace in the idea that she was no longer in pain.

The Walton kid and Doctor Ellison didn't deserve it either, but Vaughn didn't want to spend too much time thinking about them; he was sure their deaths would be all over the news for weeks to come. Kiki and the others would just be footnotes.

Suddenly, a blueish light emanated from the floor of the Doctor's office, and the sounds of Robin Thicke's "Blurred Lines" filled the halls.

The ringtone *had* to be coming from the Doctor's cell phone.

Vaughn was already on the move. If he could connect with someone — anyone — on the outside, he could tell them that the solution was in the truck downstairs. By the time he realized that nobody in their right mind would ever listen to such a crazy idea, he was already approaching the hospital gown he'd thrown as bait, when —

SKRIEEEEK!

A beast turned the corner and appeared at the end of the hall, just outside the Doctor's office. Vaughn quickly leaned up against the wall and froze. The beast hissed and shrieked again, as it turned to look inside Ellison's office.

Peering through his gas mask, Vaughn held his breath, hoping the beast was as sick of Robin Thicke as he was, and had only come to shut that awful song off.

But it turned to face Vaughn.

The beast started making a loud clicking sound that reminded Vaughn of cicadas in the summertime, only much more menacing. The piercing sound increased in tempo, when all of a sudden, the beast burst down the hall and was galloping directly towards Vaughn!

Vaughn wanted to run, but it was already upon him.

Vaughn closed his eyes.

This is it.

Vaughn was still bracing himself for the violent attack, when the clicking suddenly slowed, and he opened his eyes to see the beast hovering over the glowing hospital gown, thrusting gently. The image was disturbing. It reminded Vaughn of the kind of stuff Omar talked about watching on the weirder parts of the internet.

The beast was only a few feet away from Vaughn, but it was paying him no mind. It appeared that his presence had gone undetected. The hazmat suit worked, for now. But he had no idea how the beast might act once it finished doing whatever it was doing. It might need something to eat for dessert, Vaughn thought. Without turning his head, Vaughn scanned the hall in both directions. No sign of any other beasts. This one was alone.

Vaughn grabbed the meat cleaver tight, and quietly stepped towards the beast. His heart pounding, Vaughn stood behind the creature, which was even more hideous up close. The sporadic hairs on the beast's back looked like slimy black earthworms, and the putrid smell was seeping through his gas mask. Vaughn slowly lifted the meat cleaver to get ready to strike, but the ruffling sound of his hazmat suit caught the monster's attention.

It stopped thrusting. Vaughn froze, terrified.

Suddenly, the beast whipped around and lunged at Vaughn. It shrieked with it's jaws open, ready to consume Vaughn with its razor sharp teeth, when Vaughn closed his eyes and swung the knife across the beast's throat!

The beast's shrieks turned into a gurgle as it stumbled aside. Vaughn opened his eyes, saw the beast reeling, then quickly reared back and struck it again, this time on the back of its neck. The beast went down, but Vaughn wasn't done. His adrenaline pumping, Vaughn followed the creature so that he was standing directly above it, and began hacking away, releasing all his fear and rage and pain — from this night and beyond — directly into the flesh of the beast. Vaughn let out a barbaric war cry as specks of black fluid splattered his gas mask with each blow to the beast's body. Finally, the thing stopped moving and fell quiet.

Vaughn collapsed to his knees, his body shaking from the disorienting one-two punch of absolute dread followed by immediate exhilaration. Catching his breath, he wiped clean the lenses of his gas mask, which left him staring at a hideous beast that he'd just chopped to pieces while it was making love to a hospital gown. He expected to wake up from this nightmare any moment now...

And then Robin Thicke's voice once again filled the hall.

The Doctor's phone! Vaughn jumped up, grabbed his trusty meat cleaver and rushed into Ellison's office. He snatched up the phone, checked the screen, and felt a rush of hope surge through his body. It was an incoming call from: *"Julie, MFT, Bronx Memorial"*

Vaughn picked it up.

"Julie! It's Vaughn" he screamed.

"Vaughn? Thank God, you're okay! Are the others with you?" she asked.

Vaughn looked around the ransacked office, then peered out the gaping hole in the wall.

"They're gone," he said.

There was silence on the other end.

Vaughn stepped closer to the ledge, and looked down at the empty streets below. "Y'all made it outside?"

"Yeah, we're up the block," Julie said. "Everyone's safe. But there's not a single cop in sight."

Vaughn didn't care about that anymore.

"Head towards the Chevron station," he said.

Julie sounded confused, "The Chevron station?"

Vaughn glanced down the hall at the alien corpse and spoke into the phone with confidence, "I've got a plan."

Tom didn't know what to do. He started to grab Kiki, thinking he could pull her away so that the alien claw would come out of her, but this wasn't like removing a splinter. The arm was at least three inches thick, and still moving.

Kiki howled in pain, "Don't!"

Then Tom remembered that railroad guy they learned about in school who got an iron rod driven through his head, but he kept on living. If they pulled this thing out, Kiki might bleed to death.

Tom laid eyes on some office supplies on the pharmacist's counter, and snatched up a pair of scissors. Though they were dull as hell, Tom quickly went to work, and reached behind Kiki's back to chop the alien arm off. The beast shrieked in pain as black blood leaked from the alien's limb and down Kiki's back. Kiki was bleeding too, but Tom couldn't bare to think about that. Finally, Tom worked his way through the several inches of flesh and Kiki fell forward. The remaining part of the limb retracted through the hole in the gate.

But another reached inside — they wouldn't be safe for long.

Tom hurried to lift Kiki to her feet. Facing him, he could now see that the claw had missed her heart. It was sticking out of the right side of her chest just underneath her clavicle. Tom didn't know what organs were under there, but he knew the lungs were pretty large, and he could tell Kiki was having trouble breathing.

"Give me those," Kiki said. She snatched the scissors from Tom's hand and cut off the part of the dead alien limb that was still protruding from her chest. It dropped to the ground.

Tom rushed over to the pharmacy shelves, grabbed some peroxide and some gauze, and hurried back to Kiki. Kiki was leaning against the counter, touching the wound with her fingers, seemingly in shock at the sight of black blood. Tom opened the bottle of peroxide, and looked at Kiki.

"This is gonna hurt," he said.

He poured it on, and it immediately fizzled up with white bubbles. Kiki screamed, and Tom swiftly moved around and poured some on the back side of the wound. Kiki howled and cursed at Tom, who stayed focused.

Tom opened the roll of gauze and began wrapping Kiki from underneath her arm, and over the opposite shoulder. He wrapped it over and over, making sure to pull it tight.

Kiki yelped, and tears began spilling down her cheeks. Tom was surprised; Kiki was so tough that he was beginning to wonder if she was immune to discomfort. Thinking quickly, Tom ripped the gauze and tied it tight, then returned to the pharmacy shelves.

Prescription drugs were something Tom was familiar with, thanks to Westley. Westley was prescribed pain pills after getting a nose job during the summer of freshman year, and he was never able to get off of them. Tom was afraid to dabble, because of how quickly they became Westley's main jam, but they clearly worked to take the pain away. Within seconds, Tom returned to Kiki with bottles of OxyContin, Vicodin, and Percocet.

"Any preference?" Tom asked, as he began checking the labels for the strongest of the bunch.

"No pills," Kiki said.

Tom paused and looked up at Kiki, perplexed.

"But you're hurting…"

"If I'm going to die," Kiki said, "I wanna be conscious on my way out."

"You're not going to die," Tom said, with a confidence in his voice that he hadn't heard in years.

Tom could see Kiki appreciated his hopefulness, but the look on her face suggested she was resigned to her fate. Tom was at a loss.

"Then what do you want me to do?" he asked.

Kiki winced again, then squeezed out one word: "Music."

Tom couldn't tell if he heard Kiki right, until she pointed at her phone. Tom snatched it up, then paused to think of a song to throw on. A song came to mind immediately — it was one that his mom listened to all the time — and though he knew he could come up with something far more clever if he had the time, he quickly typed it in. A moment later, a familiar tune filled the pharmacy.

Tom glanced at Kiki to try and gauge her reaction, and he watched her small grin turn into a beaming smile as soon as Bob Marley's voice started singing the lyrics to Three Little Birds:

"Don't worry / About a thing / 'Cause everything little thing / Gonna be alright"

Kiki swayed her head gently to the beat, and she lifted her arm to give Tom a fist bump. Tom gently met her fist, and the two of them shared a look of gratitude as the tune granted them a temporary escape from their current reality. It appeared to Tom that the music was actually treating Kiki's suffering, when —

BOOM!

A beast punctured an even larger hole in the grate behind them.

"We need to get out of here," Tom said.

"Good luck with that," Kiki said, as she nodded to the door they entered through.

"What do you mean?" Tom asked, sounding terrified. "There's no back door? There's always a back door!"

Kiki shook her head, then winced, clutching her wounded chest. Tom wanted to convince Kiki that pain pills were more effective than the Bob Marley treatment, but he wondered if it was worth it. With a wound like that, she needed something stronger, something like morphine or fentanyl, the stuff they gave to wounded soldiers. But Tom also knew that stuff could kill you instantly.

Wait a second, Tom thought. *That might work!*

Overcome with excitement, Tom bolted towards the side of the pharmacy, where he spotted a small refrigerator. He opened it up and found a small rack of vials. Tom gathered the vials, snatched a box of syringes off the top of the refrigerator, then ran back to Kiki. He quickly readied the syringe, grabbed one of the vials, and began drawing medicine out of the vial and into the syringe.

"What is that?" Kiki asked.

"Fentanyl," Tom said.

Kiki shook her head, "Hell no. You rich kids are crazy."

"It's not for you," Tom said. Suddenly, Tom whipped around and jabbed it into the limb of one of the attacking beasts. He pushed the plunger down and injected the entire vial. The beast screeched and pulled its limb back, taking the syringe with it. Tom quickly grabbed another syringe, loaded it up, and jabbed the limb of a second beast that was widening a new hole in the grate. He pumped the beast full of fentanyl, but this one didn't pull it's arm back. The arm kept moving, but it started to slow down right in front of their eyes. The arm looked like it was falling asleep, and finally, it stopped moving. It slid out from the hole and they heard what sounded like a thump of the beast hitting the floor.

"I think we might be able to get out of here!" Tom shouted. He grabbed another vial, refilled the syringe, and waited for another limb to pop through the grate, like it was some kind of twisted game of whack-a-mole.

WHAM! A beast tore an opening through the grate, large enough to get its head through. Jaws wide open, the beast nearly took Tom's head off, when he reached up and jabbed the syringe into the side of the beast's head. He pushed the plunger down and the beast quickly fell back away from the gate.

Finally, Tom grabbed Kiki's phone and held up the flashlight to illuminate a hole in the grating. Peering through the hole, which looked out into the main room, he could see two beasts were slowly dragging themselves across the floor like slugs. They weren't dead, but they were vulnerable as they'd ever be.

It was now or never.

But when Tom turned back to Kiki, he noticed that she was barely able to keep her eyes open. The deep red blood stain on her hospital gown was rapidly growing in diameter. Forget making it out of this hospital, Tom thought. Kiki might not make it out of this room.

"Tom," Kiki whispered, sounding weak. "I'm not going to make it."

Tom couldn't believe what he was hearing. They locked eyes, and Tom was about to open his mouth to argue —

"Just go," she said, unyielding. "You need to save yourself."

Tom disagreed. He'd spent his whole life thinking about nobody but himself, and that hadn't gotten him anywhere. He didn't even have any real friends; Westley was more of an acquaintance than a friend, and that was only because they were both embittered, disillusioned, and nihilistic sons of rich and powerful men. Tom wondered if Westley had succeeded in getting the Dalton girls drunk enough to play truth or dare with him by now. There was nothing Westley wouldn't do for clout, especially when it came to double-dares, which in their circles meant completing a dare in exchange for a reward. Everyone in school heard about the time Westley threw a couch off the roof of his forty-story building to earn himself an original Banksy painting.

Why was Tom thinking about Westley at a time like this? He was looking into the eyes of a dying girl that he could've sworn he loved, and here he was thinking about his asshole friend partying all night on the East River, when suddenly —

An idea bubbled up.

Tom snatched up Kiki's phone, and dialed the only number he'd ever memorized outside of his dad's.

The phone rang, as Tom kept an eye on Kiki, who looked like she was going in and out of consciousness. The phone rang a second time, and Tom started getting disheartened that maybe it just wasn't meant to be, until —

A familiar voice answered.

Tom turned away from Kiki and stepped out of earshot.

"Westley, it's Tom... I've got a dare for you."

11

GOING UP

Julie sprinted up the deserted block, Omar and Mo in tow, gripping her phone in her hand. Finally, the Chevron station came into view and Julie slowed down. The three of them fought to catch their breaths.

"Okay, we're here," Julie announced into the phone. She had Vaughn on speakerphone so the others could hear.

"You see the blue and orange truck?" Vaughn asked.

They all turned to see a deteriorating box truck in the parking lot. The truck definitely has some blue paint on it, but it was hard to tell the difference between orange paint and decades-old rust spots.

"I think so," Julie said. "What about it?"

"There's something inside," Vaughn said.

Omar wondered aloud, "How the hell does he know that?"

Vaughn heard him, "I just know, Omar. Trust me."

Mo hustled over to the rear of the box truck, and found a pad lock fixed to the bottom of the roll-up gate. She held it up for the others to see.

"There's a lock on it, Vaughn," Julie told him.

Vaughn mumbled frustrated profanities from the other end.

"Y'all are square as SpongeBob," Omar said, as he walked up to Julie and pointed to a bobby pin she had in her hair.

"Can I have that?" He asked.

Curious, Julie grabbed the bobby pin and passed it over to Omar. Within seconds, he'd bent it into shape and began going to work on the lock.

Julie watched, "Hold on. Omar's doing something... illegal."

A second later, the lock popped open. Omar tossed the lock aside and turned to the crew, "Let's hope he's right."

Omar tossed the bobby pin back to Julie, then grabbed the handle of the roll-up gate, and threw it open. Julie turned on her phone's flashlight and stepped forward to inspect the interior.

"Anything in there?" Vaughn asked.

Julie's eyes went wide. So did Mo's.

"Yoooooo," Omar said with amazement, as he climbed inside.

Inside the back of the truck was an extensive arsenal of weapons. Fastened to the walls were dozens of assault rifles, grenades, and what looked like a rocket launcher. But most notably, in the center of the box truck, there was a household dishwasher strapped in place on top of a four wheel dolly. The dishwasher door had been removed, and inside the gutted appliance was an indistinguishable collection of wires, bundled plastics, and sticks of what appeared to be dynamite. The innards were illuminated by a distinct, blinking red L.E.D. inside the device that was reminiscent of a car alarm indicator, yet far more ominous given the context. A long green fuse jutted out through the open face, and next to that was a single white lighter taped to the body of the device.

Nervous, Julie spoke into the phone, "Vaughn, we found something."

"Explosives?" he asked.

"And then some," Julie replied. "This one thing looks like it could blow up an entire city block."

"That's what I need," Vaughn said, without hesitation.

Mo and Omar turned to face Julie.

"Is he serious?" Omar asked. He hopped down from the truck to get closer to the phone. "Yo Vaughn," Omar said, "There's all kinds of weapons in here bro. I can run up in there with the chopper and blow those things to pieces."

The crew stood around the phone, waiting for Vaughn's response.

"Roselle had a bomb in there for a reason," Vaughn said. "If those things came from a hole in the ground, we gotta make sure we cover it up."

"By blowing up the whole building?" Omar asked.

The trio shared a concerned look.

"You got a better idea?" Vaughn replied.

Omar thought about it. *Nope.*

Apprehensive, Mo asked, "But what if Kiki and Tom are still inside somewhere?"

"They're not," Vaughn said, definitively. "It's just me in here now."

The group glanced at the building, forlorn, when Omar noticed something strange going on a few floors up. He squinted his eyes and pointed his finger up at the hospital, "I wouldn't be so sure about that."

Julie and Mo followed Omar's eye line, and through the second floor windows, they spotted movement from a faint flashlight beam.

"Is that them!?" Mo screamed.

"Vaughn, somebody's moving on the second floor," Julie shouted.

"That was Kiki's floor!" Mo cried with excitement. "It's gotta be them!"

As the trio watched from the ground level, they could also see the beasts lurking around in the dark only a couple of windows away from the flashlight beam, on the other side of what appeared to be a wall.

"Looks like them monsters are up there too," Omar said. "If we don't do something soon, Kiki and Tom are about to become Lunchables."

Omar started to climb back into the truck, eyeing the extensive weaponry, when Vaughn spoke up, his voice full of determination:

"I'll get them out of there."

Omar paused and glanced back at the others. The trio shared a tentative look, before Omar stated what was on everybody's minds.

"Yo Vaughn, you know I got mad respect for your leadership skills and what not," Omar said, treading lightly, "But you understand how that's hard to believe given the fact that you literally just hatched a plan based on ditching them, right?"

The phone fell silent.

"That was then," Vaughn said.

"Oh, okay. So now you're gonna risk your life to save a dying girl and a rich kid that you were ready to stab an hour ago?"

"Yeah," Vaughn replied calmly. "I'm letting it go."

Omar shot a skeptical look over to Julie and Mo. Julie however, understood Vaughn's reference to their earlier conversation, and nodded with pride.

"Vaughn's got this," Julie declared, confident.

Omar and Mo were surprised by Julie's tone, but their trust in her was unshakable. They glanced up at the second floor windows, and considered Vaughn's deadly mission.

"How exactly are you gonna save them?" Omar asked into the phone. "We got all the firepower down here with us."

"Yeah, what are we supposed to do?" Mo asked. "Just stand out here and watch?"

"No," Vaughn said. "I need y'all to make a delivery."

• • •

OMAR STOOD inside the back of the box truck and pushed the button for the lift gate. The mammoth dishwasher-bomb, which had been wheeled out onto the truck's rear lift, was being lowered to the ground by the hydraulic system. Julie braced the device to keep it stable on the way down.

"Slow!" Mo yelled at Omar.

"Relax, Mo! I got this."

Omar finessed the key fob until the gate gently kissed the concrete. Julie grabbed hold of a thick strap and used all her weight to begin rolling the device off the gate and onto the sidewalk. Omar jumped down from the truck and joined Mo in keeping the bomb secure on the dolly as it trailed behind Julie.

Julie pulled the leash, and guided the dolly down the curb ramp and onto the street. She paused to look both ways, ready to cross, then turned.

"You guys ready?" Julie asked. "Let's do this quickly."

They nodded, and Julie kicked it into gear. She threw her weight into the pull and the three of them began rolling the giant bomb across the eerily empty and quiet four-lane street.

"Uh oh...," Omar said. "Not these *pendejos* again."

Julie glanced up at Omar, who was staring at something down the block. A cop car turned the corner with its flashing lights on, but no sirens. It was patrolling the street, creeping in their direction with a spotlight shining on the adjacent sidewalk.

"Go faster!" Mo yelled.

"I'm trying!," Julie yelled, and she was. But the bomb they were hauling must have weighed close to a thousand pounds.

Mo sounded like she was going to cry, "If they catch us, we're going to jail, Vaughn and Kiki and Tom are gonna die, and the aliens are gonna take over the Bronx!"

"Hey!" Julie snapped. She whipped around to face Mo, dropping the leash. "What did I teach you about catastrophizing?"

The bomb stopped rolling, as Julie stared at Mo, awaiting an answer. Mo admired how Julie never passed up an opportunity to psychoeducate.

Timidly, Mo responded, "Say stop, then focus on what *is*, and not what *ifs?*"

Julie nodded and snatched up the leash, "Good. Now PUSH!"

They continued pushing as hard as they could, but fatigue was already setting in. The trio was moving at a snails pace. Meanwhile, the police were edging closer.

Finally, Omar quit pushing. Mo and Julie looked at him, baffled.

"I'm all about the present moment, but Mo's right," Omar said. "If they see us, this whole plan fails." Omar nodded down the street at the oncoming squad car, "I need to distract them, while y'all two keep pushing."

Julie and Mo looked at one another, hesitant.

"Don't even trip," Omar said. "This right here is fun for me."

Omar gave a reassuring smile to Julie and Mo, then reached into his pocket and pulled out a grenade that he snatched from Roselle's truck. He handed it over to Julie, who looked confused.

"Come on, you never seen the ending of *I Am Legend?*" Omar asked. "You never know when a grenade might come in handy."

Julie shook her head and carefully slipped the grenade in her pocket.

"Make it happen y'all," Omar said, as he pounded his chest with his fist and started backpedaling away from them, towards the cops.

"Do it for the B-X!"

Omar threw up the infamous Bronx "X" with his crossed fore-arms, then turned around and started running towards the police.

"What's he going to do?" Mo asked.

"I don't even want to know," Julie said, then shouted, "Omar, be careful!"

But Julie knew that command was useless. She reached into

her pocket, then cautiously placed the grenade just inside the dishwasher bomb.

"Let's keep all the explosives in once place," Julie said.

Mo nodded, *good idea.*

They both looked back up at Omar, and saw him run onto the sidewalk and post up next to the liquor store. Suddenly, he dropped his pants and began urinating on the side of the building, in the exact spot they'd seen a homeless man get detained hours earlier. The giant white police spotlight glided across the brick walls, until it landed on Omar's bare ass. The spotlight stopped moving, and two officers hopped out of the car with nightsticks ready. Omar yanked up his pants and began sprinting down the street in the opposite direction, taking the police with him.

"That's his idea of *fun?*" Mo turned to Julie, "You guys might want to unpack that in your next session."

"Come on!" Julie yelled, "Now's our chance!" Julie grabbed the leash and Mo got behind the bomb, and together they used the adrenaline of the moment to begin rolling the dolly across the street. The slope of the street boosted their momentum, and within seconds, they were wheeling the bomb through the open emergency room doors of Bronx Memorial.

They pushed the bomb through the dark waiting room, which was only navigable due to the faint street light that washed in from the glass doors. Julie and Mo rolled the bomb to the elevator, and stopped.

"So how exactly is this supposed to work?" Julie asked.

"When the power dies, most commercial elevators have enough stored up juice for two or three emergency evacuation trips," Mo said. "Read it in some emergency training manual."

Julie nodded, then motioned to the elevator button. "You want to do the honors?" she asked, her voice trembling.

Mo met Julie's gaze and swallowed with fear. They could

practically hear each other's hearts pounding, both fully aware that if the elevators were dead, their entire plan was doomed.

Finally, Mo nodded and stretched her shaking finger onto the elevator button and paused.

"Any therapeutic techniques to help make this less intense?" Mo asked.

"Yeah," Julie said. "Just fucking push it."

Taken aback, Mo quickly smashed the button.

And it lit up.

Ding.

Mo cheered and turned to Julie, "Best. Therapist. Ever!"

For Tom's plan to work, Kiki needed to be mobile, which was unfortunate since Kiki could barely keep her head straight, her body noodle-like as she fought to remain upright on her chair. She was still losing blood.

Tom thought about the many times he and Westley would be on the verge of passing out at Artichoke Pizza in the middle of the night — Westley from pain pills and Tom from whatever booze he could get his hands on — and so they would start abusing Tom's ADHD medication to wake themselves up. It was dangerous as hell, and Tom knew that, but he was willing to put up with a few hours of heart palpitations if the drugs provided him with enough energy to open up the Uber app, request a ride, and get his ass home.

But this was a medical emergency. Tom could tell that there was no psychoactive drug capable of bringing Kiki back from her zombie-like state. Tom looked at Kiki and tried to assess her weight, as he wondered whether he had the strength or stamina to carry her on his back, like some sort of action hero, and fight the aliens at the same time. He quickly realized that was ridiculous. He wasn't The Rock. He wasn't Arnold. He wasn't Jason Statham.

Jason Statham. Tom had only seen one movie starring the bald British actor with the cool voice, and he would never forget it. He and his mom had planned on renting the Pixar film *Cars*, but when she was too drunk to use the remote correctly, she accidentally rented a Statham flick called *Crank*. Tom still couldn't shake the awkward feeling of being ten years-old, sitting next to his mom, and watching Statham engage in various kinds of R-rated, arousing activities to keep his adrenaline constantly flowing in order to keep himself alive. But suddenly, Tom was grateful for the movie choice — it provided him with a solution to the current dilemma.

Tom bolted back into the aisles and began scouring the shelves. Finally, he found a stack of epinephrine injectors and began ripping them from their boxes. Tom rushed back to Kiki and emerged from the aisle holding an injector in each hand.

"Ready to get out of here?" Tom asked.

Kiki rolled her head in Tom's direction.

"I think this is the end," Kiki said, her words slurring.

Tom shook his head and rushed over to Kiki. He held one of the injectors against Kiki's outer thigh, then looked up at her.

"Do I have your permission?" Tom asked. "It's adrenaline."

"Is it going to work?" Kiki asked.

Tom nodded, then mumbled under his breath, "It worked for Jason Statham."

Kiki heard the comment, but before she could ask him what he meant, Tom pushed the plunger down, sending the epinephrine into Kiki's body.

After a moment, Kiki's eyes went wide. Without warning, she quickly snatched the unused injector from Tom's other hand, and jabbed it into her opposite thigh. As she plunged the epinephrine into her muscle, her breath rate increased, and her posture began to straighten.

Suddenly, Kiki hopped down off the counter and landed on her feet. Tom was startled by the rapid shift, figuring that *Crank* had to be an exaggeration of reality. But Kiki was already shifting back and forth, looking intensely wired. Tom felt a little nervous, especially when he realized that he hadn't even checked the dosage. Not that he would have known what an appropriate amount of epinephrine was; it wasn't the sort of drug people casually talked about doing at parties.

"Kiki, maybe we should chill here for a second," Tom cautioned.

"Hell no, I'm ready to crack some freakin' heads!" she roared. In one swift motion, Kiki grabbed her phone, snatched the pair of scissors off the counter, and yanked open the pharmacy door to confront the monsters.

"Kiki, no!" Tom yelled.

But before she could step outside, a frenzied beast barreled over her.

12

THE FINAL DISPLAY

Tom watched Kiki land flat on her back, and through the shadows he could see a large, blurred figure towering over her. Tom quickly grabbed a chair, lifted it over his head, and was about to strike when the figure suddenly turned around on two feet and slammed the door closed.

Tom froze. This wasn't a beast. In fact, it looked more like a ghost; it was white from head to toe. *What the hell was going on in this place?*

Suddenly, the figure turned to Tom, "You can put that down now."

The voice was immediately recognizable, and Tom's hunch was confirmed when Vaughn removed his gas mask and lowered the hood of his hazmat suit. Tom dropped the chair, relieved, as Vaughn reached out a hand and yanked Kiki to her feet.

"You good?" Vaughn asked a stunned Kiki.

"Yeah, I'm freaking great," she said, talking at a blistering speed. "But you kinda ruined my moment. I was about to bash those things' heads in."

"They would've eaten you alive," Vaughn said. He noticed the gnarly wound on Kiki's chest and quickly pulled up a chair. "You should sit."

Without debate, Kiki plopped down. Her mind and body vacillating between energized and exhausted.

"How come they didn't eat *you*?" Tom asked Vaughn.

Vaughn turned to Tom and chuckled, "Sorry to disappoint you, Tom."

"Na, I didn't mean it like that —-"

"It's alright if you did... I kinda deserve it," Vaughn said, primarily to himself. Tom and Kiki looked confused by the comment, and Vaughn remembered that he was the only one in the room aware of the fact that he'd planned on abandoning the two of them earlier in order to save his own ass. But this was no time to ask for forgiveness.

"To answer your question," Vaughn said, "Some of that glowing stuff rubbed off on me. But realized that if I covered the smell of it, the beasts wouldn't be able to track me."

"So you just walked right past them?" Tom asked.

"Not exactly. They were moving kinda slow out there to be honest —"

"That was the fentanyl," Kiki interjected. She gave Tom a high-five, then clarified for Vaughn, "Tom drugged them from in here."

Vaughn nodded at Tom, his way of saying *nice work*. Tom appreciated the subtle acknowledgment.

"They're still moving though, so I threw some bait down the hall to get them away from the doors. They're getting busy with my hospital gown."

Tom and Kiki looked confused. Vaughn realized it would take too long to try and explain the details of alien sexual behavior.

"Forget it," Vaughn said.

"Are the others okay?" Kiki asked.

Vaughn nodded, "They made it out. But listen, we don't have much time. We've got to get to the elevators while they're still distracted."

Tom was perplexed, "You do know there's a power outage, right?"

"The elevators are still running," Vaughn said. "And the one at the end of the hallway has a bomb inside."

Trying his best to be diplomatic, Tom tried to reason with Vaughn, "Now I know you kinda have a fondness for explosives, and I totally respect that, like no judgment at all, but I wonder if it might better for us to search for a way out of the building instead of trying to blow it up."

Vaughn shook his head. "It's the only way... All three of us have that stuff on us. They're going to follow us wherever we go."

Tom looked over at Kiki and noticed for the first time that she too had managed to get the glowing substance on the back of her hospital gown. Tom was confused as to how or when that could've happened, until he remembered that they had crept down the hallway back-to-back on their way to Ellison's office. The three of them shared a look. Kiki immediately understood what needed to be done. Tom, on the other hand, appeared hesitant.

Vaughn noticed, and spoke directly to Tom, "I know you're probably gonna go back to where you're from, back to where it's safe, and maybe those creatures won't get you over there. But you've seen how it works here. Nobody's coming to help people like us. If you wanna leave, then leave. I can't get mad about self-preservation. I just want you to ask yourself; are you going to be able to sleep at night knowing that you ran away from a chance to do the right thing?"

Tom held Vaughn's stare for an extended beat, and when he glanced over at Kiki, he was struck by the overwhelming sense of closeness he felt not just to them, but to all five of the strangers he came to know over the course of the night. Something about each of them felt undeniably real. They wore no masks. They played no roles. They were just real. Tom didn't know whether to attribute it to the psych ward, or the sharing of a near-death experience, or the no-bullshit nature of the Bronx, but he decided that if he somehow managed to survive this ordeal, he wanted to figure out how to meet people like them without needing to be involuntarily committed. He'd probably have to get out of Manhattan, Tom thought, since it appeared to him that the price of comfort and privilege was a loss of truth and humanity.

Tom knew there was something happening within him that was going beyond thoughts of self-preservation. Maybe it was what Kiki had said earlier about Darwin; maybe he *was* connected to something bigger than himself, connected to the long-term survival of the human species. Whatever it was, Tom knew he couldn't leave Bronx Memorial until those things were destroyed.

His heart pounding, Tom looked at Vaughn and shook his head side to side. He quickly followed up the response with a question:

"So... what's the plan?"

Vaughn and Kiki looked moved by Tom's commitment to their mission. But the heartwarming moment was short lived.

"The plan is," Vaughn replied, "We draw them close to the bomb..."

Vaughn paused to clear his throat.

"And end this."

The room fell silent.

There was nothing else to say.

Vaughn was perched on the pharmacy counter, shining the Doctor's phone flashlight through one of the holes in the gate to scan the room outside. He spotted the outlines of several creatures, swelling up and down with each monstrous breath.

"They're still over near the opposite wall," Vaughn said.

He turned around to find Tom helping Kiki to her feet, her arm around Tom's shoulder.

Tom was taken aback by how much effort it was taking to support Kiki. She wasn't heavy, but her body wasn't able to do any of the work. Kiki moaned in pain.

"You okay?" Tom asked. Kiki looked like she was fading, fast. Apparently, adrenaline was no match for this sort of blood loss. Tom glanced at Vaughn, the two of them wearing looks of concern. Both of them knew there was no way Kiki was going to outrun a trio of killer aliens down the two-hundred foot corridor leading to the elevator.

And so did Kiki.

"You guys have to leave me here," she said.

Tom and Vaughn locked eyes again, and together, they shook their heads. They were finally on the same page. But what the hell were they going to do? Carry her? Give her a freaking piggy back ride down the hall? They could each grab one of Kiki's arms and drag her, but that would slow all of them down. Too bad they couldn't throw her in a shopping cart or something and push her —

There's an idea, Tom thought.

Tom snatched Kiki's phone, and shined the flashlight around the room.

"Vaughn, could you grab her real quick?"

Vaughn hopped down from the counter and Tom handed Kiki off.

Tom began frantically searching around the pharmacy, until finally, he found what he was looking for. He scooped up a large, shiny object, then rushed back to Vaughn and Kiki.

Tom slammed it down and opened it up.

A wheelchair.

"Oh, you're definitely coming with us now," Vaughn said, as he carefully lowered Kiki into the chair.

Together, Vaughn and Tom strapped Kiki in, then stood up to face one another.

"I'll push her," Tom said.

"You sure?" Vaughn asked.

"You're the fastest one here," Tom said. "If something happens to us, you still need to get to that bomb."

Vaughn considered this for a moment, then nodded. It made sense. Besides, there was no time for discussion. Vaughn stepped towards the door, and Tom got into position behind Kiki's wheelchair.

"Guys, wait" Kiki said. They both looked at Kiki to find her extending one hand towards Tom, and the other towards Vaughn, palms facing up. Vaughn wasted no time and quickly placed his hand on top of Kiki's. Both of them turned to look at Tom. It took a second for Tom to register what was being proposed. Tom had never prayed before, but he figured he had nothing to lose. He grasped Kiki's hand.

"Yo," Vaughn said, getting Tom's attention. Tom saw that Vaughn was extending his free hand towards him. Tom assumed that the Bible must have claimed that a prayer circle needs to be a closed circuit in order for the old man in the sky to receive distress signals. It wasn't any more far fetched than the idea of subterranean aliens invading a hospital in the Bronx. So Tom reached out and joined hands with Vaughn.

Kiki bowed her head, closed her eyes.

"Dear God, give us the strength to carry out this mission ahead. If it's our time to leave this world, we ask that you allow us to go peacefully, knowing that we did the best that we could. If we survive, allow us to continue acting as vehicles for spreading light and spreading love. Thank you for bringing us together to defeat this evil, and let us help each other to survive, tonight and forevermore. Amen."

Kiki opened her eyes.

"Amen," Vaughn echoed. He opened his eyes and dropped his hands.

Something came over Tom, and as soon as he opened his eyes, words came tumbling out, "I just want to say thank you."

Kiki and Vaughn turned to look at him, unsure of whether he was talking to them or to God.

"To you guys," Tom said. "For waking me up."

SCREECH! The trio recoiled as an alien cried out from the main room. Those wicked things sure know how to ruin a moment, Tom thought.

"I'm not saying you're welcome," Vaughn said, nodding towards the noise. "Not until we blow those things to pieces."

Vaughn and Tom exchanged smirks, then Vaughn turned to grab the doorknob. Tom readied himself behind Kiki's wheelchair.

"Hey Tom," Kiki said, weakly. "Do, do me a favor?"

Vaughn paused, and Tom leaned over to look at Kiki, who was putting her bulky bluetooth headphones over her ears.

"Put on the theme song from *'Last of the Mohicans'.*" Kiki pointed to her phone, which Tom was still holding in his hand.

It was a weird request, but Tom wasn't about to deny Kiki of what might be her final wishes. He quickly punched the song into Spotify, saw the cover art of Daniel Day Lewis looking like a native warrior, and hit play.

Kiki gave a thumbs up.

"Here," Tom said, passing the phone back to Kiki so that she could illuminate the way with her flashlight. Kiki steadied the light on her lap.

The epic tune leaked out of the headphones, filling the quiet room. Vaughn glanced back at Tom and they locked eyes.

Ready?

They shared a nod.

Took a deep breath.

And Vaughn pushed the door open.

Vaughn was off and running — already turning into the corridor by the time Tom and Kiki fully emerged from the pharmacy.

Tom spotted the beasts immediately.

On the far side of the main room, the trio of beasts were huddled together, an undulating mass of dark hair hovering above a glowing red cloth. Tom felt a glimmer of hope that they might remain distracted in their hospital gown fetish, when suddenly, as if hearing Tom's optimism, they whipped around.

The beasts *SHRIEKED* and *HISSED*, and when the cell phone's light glistened off three sets of carnivorous, blood-stained teeth, Tom's adrenaline got to pumping. Before he knew it, his legs had already taken him and Kiki halfway down the hall.

Tom didn't know how far behind him they were, but he could hear that the snarls, clicks, and hisses were getting louder. Kiki, who was holding the light steady in her wheelchair, craned her neck to look over her shoulder —

"FASTER!" She screamed, her voice more shrill than ever.

Oh crap, Tom thought. They must be close.

Tom could see Vaughn up ahead, closing in on the elevator. Miraculously, just as Vaughn had promised, the digital display above the closed door revealed a red "2." He watched Vaughn punch the button on the wall, and the elevator doors opened to reveal the hefty explosive parked on four wheels.

Vaughn stepped into the elevator and quickly found the lighter that was taped to the side of the device. He ripped it free and began searching for the fuse.

Tom kicked it into a gear that he never knew he possessed. It wasn't the sight of the bomb; it was the sudden realization that his own plan could still work alongside Vaughn's — they weren't mutually exclusive. Tom didn't regret not bringing it up back in the pharmacy, because he knew it wouldn't have gone over well. It would have sounded crazy. It was the kind of thing that had to be sprung onto somebody last minute, before they could pick apart the logic.

Tom and Kiki were less than twenty feet away from the elevator, when Vaughn turned around to look at them, eyes wide.

Vaughn was sweating bullets, and Tom could tell that he was panicked. The monsters had to be right behind him, Tom thought, when —

BOOM!

Tom didn't know what happened, but he suddenly found himself face down on the floor. He'd been hit with such force from behind that it sent Kiki's wheel chair catapulting towards the elevator. Tom tried to pick himself up, but his shoulder hurt like hell, and he saw blood pouring down his arm.

Then he heard the hissing...

Tom could feel the breath of one of the beasts hitting the back of his neck, and the smell of rotted flesh made him gag. Tom didn't even care to turn over and look at the hideous thing. He decided he'd rather die with a final image of a hallway, at the end of which sat a girl he might have loved, and a boy he grew to understand.

Tom braced himself the inevitable the death blow, when he heard the beast *SQUEAL*. Tom felt a hot liquid dripping down the back of his neck, and when he opened his eyes, he saw only Kiki in front of the elevator. He heard the beast cry out again, and Tom flipped over to see Vaughn holding onto a bloody meat cleaver, and the beast recoiling with a gash in its abdomen.

"That's not a peaceful way to go," Vaughn said to him. Using his free hand, Vaughn yanked Tom to his feet, and Tom dashed ahead to the elevator.

Tom slipped past Kiki, who had managed to wheel herself inside the elevator, and turned to face the hall. Over Vaughn's shoulder, Tom saw that two of the beasts were slowly trailing behind their wounded leader, and he assumed they must be the hospital's newest fentanyl addicts. But it was clear that the beasts were going to follow them no matter where they went. So Tom immediately reached out and punched a button.

Vaughn leapt into to the elevator, got down on his knee, and pulled out the lighter. He started to light the fuse, but stopped when he noticed the elevator doors starting to close.

"What the—!?" Vaughn jumped up, and reached out for the door sensors to keep them open, when Tom grabbed Vaughn and held him back.

"Stop! What are you doing?!" Vaughn screamed.

With the beasts only a few feet away, Vaughn struggled desperately to break free from Tom, as the elevator the doors closed shut. The beasts smashed into the steel doors, and the elevator started going up, pulling away from the threat.

Finally, Vaughn slipped out of Tom's hold, then whipped around and grabbed him by the throat. Vaughn threw him into the wall, "That was our one chance to kill those things! Do you *want* them to live?!"

The elevator beeped, and the display showed an illuminated arrow pointing up, next to the floor number: "3"

Tom shook his head profusely, "No, you just gotta trust me."

"Trust you!? You just ruined our plan!"

Kiki remained quiet, as her tired eyes peered into the inside of the dishwasher bomb. The placement of her wheelchair gave her a front row view of the bomb's innards.

The elevator beeped again, the display reading: "4"

"We're still going to kill them, I promise," Tom said. "There's just something I've got to do first."

Tom took the phone from Kiki's weak hands, and started punching buttons.

"Something *you've* got to do first," Vaughn was seething. "There it is again, that selfish gene. It's all about you! Let me guess... you're having second thoughts about destroying your dad's building. Worried about your futures investments, is that it?"

Glued to Kiki's phone, Tom just shook his head. The elevator beeped, and stopped moving. The display read: RF.

The elevator doors opened to the large rooftop. Tom looked

up from the phone to see construction materials and debris scattered across the roof. It was being demolished, just as Kiki had said.

Tom wheeled Kiki out of the elevator, then returned to grab a hold of the leash attached to the bomb's dolly.

He looked at Vaughn, "You gonna help me or not?"

Vaughn didn't know what to say.

"It's the same plan, just with a view," Tom said. "I promise."

Vaughn shook his head, dumbfounded —

BANG! They turned to see the rooftop's staircase door was being introduced to the strength of the beasts. The beasts had followed their scent, just as Tom had hoped.

Trust or not, Vaughn grabbed the leash with Tom and they rolled the dolly out underneath the night sky and into the center of the rooftop. Tom quickly ran back to grab Kiki, and wheeled her towards the bomb. He positioned her seat so that she was facing the skyline of Manhattan, then grabbed the phone.

Kiki and Vaughn looked at one another, confused. The view was spectacular, but they were both worried that Tom had lost his mind under pressure. The beasts were thrashing against the rooftop door, yet Tom didn't seem concerned.

"Alright, no more games," Vaughn said. "What's this about?"

Tom typed out a text that read: "*NOW,*" and hit *SEND.*

Tom passed the phone back to Kiki, then looked up at them both.

"It's not about me."

That didn't clear things up, but Tom preferred to let his actions do the explaining. *Come on, Westley. Please don't screw this up.* Tom waited anxiously, and the heavy weight of doubt and despair began to creep in. He wondered if he had once again been let down by his "friend," even after guaranteeing Westley the keys to his father's yacht in exchange for pulling off this outrageous stunt.

Suddenly, something sounding like a rocket caught their

attention in the night sky. Seconds later, a gigantic red, white, and blue firework exploded over the East River. And then another. And then the entire Macy's fireworks display was suddenly taking place a day ahead of time, thanks to his clout-obsessed, transactional acquaintance.

The trio stood together, their faces aglow as they watched the fireworks explode in the sky, the three of them sharing a moment of awestruck splendor. The rage fell away from Vaughn's face as he realized Tom's plan was anything but selfish. Vaughn knew about Kiki's love for fireworks; she'd told the group on several occasions. Vaughn glanced over at Tom, who was awaiting his gaze. Vaughn couldn't help but chuckle, amazed at what Tom had accomplished. There were no words exchanged, but Vaughn's gratified nod was a tacit acknowledgment that Tom had been forgiven.

Kiki, who was seated next to Tom, leaned over and rested her head on his arm, her teary eyes fixed on the mesmerizing sky. Tom looked down at her, and she glanced at Tom for a second to mouth the words, "Thank you."

Her eyes floated back to the rainbow colored sky, and Tom put his arm around Kiki's shoulder. It felt easy and natural. It felt authentic. He could care for a member of the opposite sex, without lusting over them. Such a thing was possible.

Tom looked back up at the majestic show, thinking about Kiki's words from earlier. Despite our differences, Tom thought, we all share the same sky. Something about that idea was so simple, yet it was impossible for him to grasp prior to tonight.

BOOM! Not even the explosions above them could mask the fury of the beasts. Tom and Vaughn turned to see the beasts were pounding on the rooftop door, altering its shape as if it were made of clay and not metal. The hinges were shaking loose.

"Yo, I hate to kill the vibe," Vaughn said, "But we still got a job to do."

Finally, Kiki peeled her eyes from the vibrant display and refocused on the current situation. They all nodded in agreement.

Tom got behind Kiki's wheelchair and pushed it closer to the bomb. Vaughn followed along, and pulled out the lighter.

"Oh, before I forget," Tom said. "We're gonna survive this."

Tom pointed to the construction debris chute on the side of the roof. Kiki had completely forgotten about the very information that she had shared with Tom earlier. The rooftop construction was a way out. Vaughn looked energized and suddenly hopeful.

"We just need to light this and bail. Kiki, maybe you wanna get a head start," Tom said.

Kiki reached for Tom to help her our of the wheelchair. She was able to steady herself, the adrenaline levels increasing with the sudden possibility of survival. She began to hobble towards the edge of the roof, as Tom remained with Vaughn for moral support. Vaughn flicked the lighter.

"You should go too," Vaughn said.

"No way. I should be the one to light it," Tom said.

Vaughn shook his head. "We're not doing the 'white savior' thing bro. Not tonight."

"I'm not the savior of this story," Tom said. "You guys are. Besides, I've had enough handicaps already."

Vaughn looked at Tom with respect, then passed the lighter over and stood up.

"I'll see you down there," Vaughn said.

"Hopefully," Tom responded.

Vaughn hurried over to Kiki and helped her move towards the side of the roof.

Tom knelt down next to the bomb and searched for the fuse, when —

BOOM! Tom looked up to see the top hinge on the rooftop door had come loose. The monsters were clawing at the metal, bending the opening so that they could squeeze though. It was only a matter of seconds.

"LIGHT IT! NOW!" Vaughn screamed from the side of the roof.

Tom was sweating, his hands shaking. He flicked the lighter, but it didn't catch. He tried again, and got nothing but sparks. He couldn't get it lit.

Tom took a deep breath, said *"please help me"* to whatever entity might hear him, then thumbed the lighter one more time.

And it fired up. Tom moved the flame to the fuse, and it caught. Sparks flew, and the distinct fizzling sound gave Tom confidence.

Tom jumped up, took about ten steps towards the debris chute, when he heard the fizzling sound stop. Tom slammed the breaks and turned around.

The fuse had gone out.

Before Tom could react, Kiki rushed past him towards the bomb.

"Kiki, what are you doing?!" Vaughn yelled.

Tom looked at the lighter in his hand, also confused. Tom chased her back to the bomb, and saw her kneel down to grab something off the bomb. When Tom arrived, he knelt down next to Kiki, and she turned to him, wincing in pain, holding a grenade in her hand.

"Tom, you need to go," she said.

Tom was baffled. He had no idea where the grenade came from, and was clueless of the fact that Kiki had formulated this back-up plan during their elevator ride up, when she made the discovery of the stray explosive.

Tom held out the lighter, "But we can just light it again —"

Kiki shook her head, "If it goes out, we're all screwed."

"Then I'll stay with you, and we'll pull the pin and —-"

"Tom! Just go," Kiki pleaded. "You and Vaughn need to survive this. You have your whole lives ahead of you. You can still try to make things right in this world."

BOOM! The rooftop door slammed to the ground, and the three beasts came charging across the roof.

"You're a good kid, Tom Walton." Kiki stood up, placed her hands on Tom's temples, and in a maternal gesture, she gently kissed the top of his head. Kiki looked Tom in the eyes and said, "Your mom would be proud."

Tom was deeply moved. He stood there speechless.

"Hey Siri, play *Dancing Queen* by ABBA," Kiki smiled at Tom as Siri went searching. "I talked the talk," she shrugged. "Now I've gotta dance the dance."

With no further warning, Kiki slipped her headphones on and pulled the pin on the grenade.

"Now go!" Kiki screamed and pushed Tom away.

Tom fell back, but remained frozen in place.

"GO!" She screamed at him again, the tone in her voice firm. Kiki spun around in an artful twist to face the oncoming beasts.

Reluctantly, Tom turned and ran towards Vaughn, who was waiting at the entrance of the debris chute. Vaughn was staring over Tom's shoulder, looking awestruck. As Tom neared the edge of the roof, he stopped to look back.

The two boys watched Kiki in the middle of the roof, dancing around the bomb, grenade in hand. For Tom, it was another one of those moments that seemed to alter time; it slowed down to a crawl. The sight was dreamlike, with fireworks of red, white, and blue illuminating Kiki's elegant body as it twirled around gracefully to music only she could hear. The angelic performance was at odds with the surrounding hellscape, which now featured rapidly approaching, salivating beasts. The monsters closed in around Kiki, when all of a sudden —

KA-MOTHERFUCKING-BOOM!

The two boys were knocked down the debris chute, as the shock wave of a massive explosion swept across the roof. A fireball illuminated the path as the boys slid down the dark tunnel, like some nightmarish amusement ride.

The earth shook and rumbled as the chute carried the boys away from the collapsing building, and when they hit the ground, they disappeared into the dust.

And that was all that was left of Bronx Memorial Hospital.

13

THE "X"

Tom coughed and wiped dust from his eyes. He looked around, and through the thick air particles he could see that he had landed in a dumpster full of rubble and trash bags across the street from the hospital.

Tom had no idea how long he'd been out. The last thing he remembered was seeing Kiki engulfed by a blast of white light that threw him backwards down the debris chute.

"Yo Tom, you alive?"

Tom turned in the direction of the labored voice to find Vaughn slowly sitting up, his face caked in grey grime.

"I think so," Tom said. "That, or the afterlife ran out of Swiffers."

Vaughn chuckled and they shared a look of mutual appreciation. Finally, Vaughn stood up and offered Tom a hand. Tom grabbed on and Vaughn yanked him up to his feet. Together, they climbed down from the dumpster and landed on the sidewalk, which was covered in an inch of soot. The particles continued falling around them in a blizzard of ash.

They heard footsteps approaching, and through the mist, they could make out two figures advancing toward them. Vaughn and Tom froze, not trusting anything that moved.

"I think I see them!" A female voice exclaimed, before Julie and Mo emerged from the ashy haze.

"You did it! You guys freaking did it!" Mo screamed, as she jumped up to hug Vaughn, then Tom. She couldn't contain her excitement, but her demeanor shifted when she readied herself for a third embrace, only to discover that Kiki was nowhere in sight.

"Is it just you two?" Mo inquired.

The boys nodded solemnly.

"But we didn't do this," Tom said, then nodded up to where the hospital once stood, "Kiki did."

Mo's face puckered, and tears started to well up.

"And she went out like a true queen," Vaughn added.

That last bit of information seemed to bring Mo some solace. She rubbed her watery eyes, then turned towards the mountain of ash where the hospital used to be, and cupped her hands around the sides of her mouth.

"I LOVE YOU KIKI!" Mo screamed at the top of her lungs. Her voice echoed off the surrounding brick walls, sounding like a hundred different fans of Kiki expressing their gratitude. Everybody listened, the moment bittersweet.

"Can we all do that?" Tom asked.

They all looked at Tom and nodded. Tom cupped his hands around his mouth, and the others followed.

Tom lead the count, "One, two, three!"

In unison, the four of them screamed, "I LOVE YOU KIKI!" The words went booming through the air, four times as loud, four times the echo. They stood and listened until the very last echo faded into silence. The small tribute seemed to bring each of them a sense of relief.

Julie stepped forward and hugged the two boys at the same time.

"I'm so proud of you two," she said, squeezing them tight. Julie pulled back and looked to Tom.

"I know it might be hard to believe," Julie said, "But the Bronx isn't normally this crazy."

Police sirens wailed in the distance. Everybody turned towards the sound.

"*Now* they come," Vaughn remarked.

"Maybe it's the ones who got Omar," Mo said.

Concerned, Tom asked,"What happened to Omar?"

"Gave himself up for the cause," Julie said. "You guys make one hell of a team, believe it or not."

The red and blue flashing lights fought their way through the thick brown air, and a police car came to a screeching halt.

And then a second.

And third.

Behind them, they heard car doors slamming and people yelling to one another. A gust of wind cleared the air for a moment to reveal dozens of journalists and cameramen setting up tripods in front of their news trucks.

"FREEZE!"

Tom and the others spun around to find several police officers emerging from the dust with their guns drawn, while others began setting up a barricade to restrain the crowding journalists.

Vaughn, Mo and Julie all had their hands in the air. Tom, however, figured this had to be some kind of sick joke.

"PUT YOUR HANDS IN THE AIR, NOW!"

It was hard to tell which officer was yelling, since they all looked identical; clean shaven, light ruddy skin, square jaws. The crew glared at Tom, urging him to follow directions.

But Tom just shook his head.

"You guys are shitting me, right?" Tom asked, incredulous. "We just saved all of your lives, and you're going to point guns at us?"

"Tom, don't get me killed after all this," Vaughn said. "Just put them up."

Tom saw the fear in Vaughn's face and quickly recognized that he was underestimating the current threat. Reluctantly, Tom put his hands in the air. It felt unnatural, because it was. Only other time he'd put his hands up was when DJs at Coachella told him to do do.

"Step away from Mister Walton, now!"

Huh?

They all turned to one another. No way they heard that correctly.

"Put your hands behind your heads and step forward!"

Vaughn, Mo, and Julie followed directions, and walked towards the police. As soon as they reached them, the police lowered their guns and yoked them up. The officers quickly threw cuffs around the trio, leaving Tom standing there by himself, confused and enraged.

"What the hell are you doing?! They didn't do anything!" He yelled. Tom tried to rush forward, when a tall officer stepped forward, blocking his path.

"It's okay son," the officer said. "Your father filled us in. You're safe now."

"My father?" Tom asked. "Is he even *here*?"

The officer didn't know how to answer that, but his reaction made the answer to that question very clear.

Of course not, Tom thought.

Tom's brain was short circuiting. He couldn't believe the people who'd just saved his life — and many others — were being shackled and escorted into squad cars.

Tom knew he couldn't let it happen.

"I blew up this building!" Tom shouted.

The officer looked puzzled.

"I despise my dad's behavior, so I wrecked his new investment." Tom knew that nobody would believe the alien story, not even from someone of his pedigree, but a bitter son destroying his father's property, maybe. Tom had learned a lot about privilege over the course of the evening, and figured he'd might as well use it.

The officer turned and whistled to his brothers in blue, who were restraining the three suspects. He put up his hand for them to halt.

"Those people are innocent!" Tom yelled. He looked around and pronounced loudly for the world to hear, "This whole thing was my doing. I hate what my dad is doing with his development projects, so I wanted to take a stand. This is me turning myself in."

Everybody heard it. Vaughn, Mo, and Julie were shocked and impressed by the story Tom had concocted on the fly to ensure their freedom. The journalists also caught wind of the drama, and were rushing forward to try and get some words with the Walton boy.

Tom had his hands out, ready to be cuffed, when he spotted the familiar face of journalist Dom Willis from *The New York Chronicle*. After witnessing the journalist's interaction with his father earlier in the evening outside of Bond Street Grill, the man's identity was burned into his memory. That's when Tom realized he had something in his pocket that had somehow survived the ordeal. He reached into his pants pocket and pulled out the tape recorder, the one that had captured his father's offensive interaction with the passionate journalist.

"Sorry about my dad," Tom said, before tossing the recorder over to the journalist. "This is the least I can do."

The journalist looked bemused. He quickly hit the rewind button and pushed play, and heard the Senator Walton's denigrating words, "*...If poor people got off their lazy asses and worked harder, maybe they wouldn't have to scrape by, living as a bottom feeder like you!... Fucking animals.*"

The journalist stopped the recording and looked at Tom, exhilarated by the magnitude of what he now possessed. Dom

Willis from *The New York Chronicle* quickly shoved the recorder in his pocket, and rushed off to his news truck.

Tom turned back to the officer and held his hands out, but the officer calmly escorted Tom by the arm towards the squad cars. Tom didn't *want* to be cuffed, but he could feel how differently he was being treated from the rest of the crew, and he couldn't help but laugh.

It was all so blatant.

"Let them go," the tall officer told his lackeys, who were restraining Vaughn, Mo, and Julie. They began removing the cuffs from the trio's wrists as Tom was escorted past them.

"Tom, what are you doing?" Vaughn asked.

Tom beamed, "Being part of the solution."

The appreciation on Vaughn's face was unmistakable. In solidarity, Vaughn smiled and pounded his chest with his fist. The reaction filled Tom with an unfamiliar sense of warmth, meaning, and purpose, as he was shoved into the back of a squad car.

The officer slammed the door closed, and Tom peered out the back window of the squad car at his new friends. That's when he saw Vaughn throwing up the "X" in Tom's direction. Tom wanted to return the gesture, but knew it wasn't his to play with. And then Vaughn pointed at Tom and gave him a nod of permission. Tom suddenly understood that the "X" was more than a gesture that repped where you were from; it was a sign of what you stood for. It was reserved for those who lived true. And Tom felt honored to be gifted this accolade. Delighted, Tom raised his forearms to the window and threw up the "X."

Tom and Vaughn shared a smile until Tom's view was cut off by dozens of reporters who swooped in, snapping photos of him in the back of the car.

Tom lowered his arms and reflected upon the chaotic scene, and he was suddenly overcome with emotions. A part of him wanted to cry. Another part wanted to laugh. Other parts wanted to scream, dance, fight, and love. But most importantly, Tom knew that deep down, every single part of him wanted to live.

Tom Walton stood with his forehead pressed against the glass of his bedroom window on East 155th Street, peering out at the New York City skyline from the Bronx side of the river. His eyes looked especially hopeful for a young man who was only a week out from having spent his seventeenth birthday surviving an alien invasion.

A knock at the door snapped Tom from his trance.

Tom turned to see Rosa opening the bedroom door.

"Mister Walton," she started, before Tom corrected her —

"It's Tom," he said. "No more of that Mister Walton stuff."

Rosa nodded, looking pleasantly surprised by his transformation.

"Tom," she said. "Your new roommates have arrived. The U-Haul is downstairs."

"Thanks Rosa," Tom said, as he moved towards the door. "Also, I was serious about what I said. Your name's on the lease, but you don't work for me anymore. Think about what you want to do, and I'll support you. Going back to school, teaching dance, or sitting around getting massages every day... Whatever it is, I've got you."

Rosa reached out and gave Tom a hug.

"You know," Rosa said, "I wished this for you."

Tom pulled away and looked at Rosa, touched.

"Hopefully not the alien part," Tom joked.

Rosa smiled and shook her head, "No. Just the kindness."

Tom gave Rosa another hug, then slipped past her and stepped into the living room of his modest Bronx apartment. Telemundo was blaring a news story in Spanish, and Tom wasn't surprised to see his father's disgraced face on the TV screen. Eyes cast down, the former Senator ashamedly announced his resignation after a recording of an offensive rant about the underprivi-leged was leaked on the internet, and subsequently went viral. Tom paid the program no mind as he crossed the room, and left the apartment.

Tom bounded down the stairs, an excited spring in every step. He finally reached the ground floor, which had no door-man, and pushed open the front doors to find Vaughn, Omar, Julie and Mo standing on the sidewalk, next to an open U-Haul van.

"There he is," Omar said. "The newest Bronx White."

"Darn skippy, son," Tom said playfully.

The group exchanged greetings in the form of hugs and pounds. Everybody was genuinely enthusiastic to be reunited.

Tom turned to Mo and Omar. "Your rooms are all ready," he said, before motioning to the U-Haul van, "Shall we?"

"Can we see the place first?" Mo asked.

Tom nodded and tossed the keys to Mo, "Apartment four-two-one. And be nice to Rosa, she's going to be our legal guardian... since Julie refused."

Tom smirked at Julie, who playfully threw her hands up, "Hey, I would if I could. But I'm pretty sure the licensing board wouldn't dig that arrangement."

"You and your damn ethics," Vaughn said, to which the group chuckled.

Mo dangled the keys with excitement, "Who's coming with me?" She asked, then skipped to the front door.

Omar and Julie followed behind her.

"We'll start unloading the stuff," Vaughn said.

"No doubt," Omar said, backpedaling into the lobby. "Be careful with my DVD's though. I got some vintage Jenna Jameson joints in there that are worth heavy dough."

Vaughn and Tom playfully waved him off, and Omar disap-peared into the building behind the others.

The boys looked at each other for a beat. Tom couldn't help

but notice that every day life was sometimes even more uncomfortable than an alien invasion.

"I appreciate you doing this for Mo and Omar," Vaughn said. "Makes me happy knowing you're gonna be living together."

"Of course... if you ever want to move in, let me know."

"I'm good, thanks," Vaughn said. "Y'all got me realizing how lucky I am to have my mom around. Spending every second I can with her."

Tom praised the comment with a spirited nod.

The two of them stood there in silence, both in a state of deep reflection.

"So... how are you doing?" Vaughn asked Tom, to his surprise.

"I'm...," Tom was about to respond, when he realized he hadn't thought about how he was doing. So much had happened. Hiring lawyers. Outing his father. Converting his stocks. Switching schools. Moving to the Bronx. Kiki's funeral...

"You really cared about her, didn't you?" Vaughn asked.

Tom tilted his head, his gaze cast down, as he searched for the right response. A mournful look washed over him as his head started to nod.

"Hey," Vaughn held out his open hand, offering up a pound. Tom reached out and returned the handshake, in a pound that popped loud, and Vaughn pulled him in tight.

"Kiki taught us something we can't forget," Vaughn said. "No matter what happens. You just gotta keep it moving."

It was true, Tom thought. Kiki dropped so many nuggets of wisdom that night, it was hard to keep track.

Tom and Vaughn completed the handshake — their index and pointer fingers snapping off one another's like they'd been practicing it for years — when suddenly, just over Vaughn's shoulder, Tom saw a white van with dark tints come screeching to a halt in the street. The doors popped open, and four figures dressed in all black, wearing hoodie balaclavas to conceal their faces, jumped out of the van with guns drawn.

Tom immediately threw his hands up, and when Vaughn whipped around, he did the same.

Curiously, the figures were not pointing their assault rifles at Tom and Vaughn. Instead, the gunners were scanning their surroundings, making sure the area was safe, before one of them waved back to someone inside the van.

A tall, imposing figure emerged. The figure was dressed similarly to the others, but sported an orange, white and blue flag that was draped over their shoulders like a sash. Vaughn had seen those colors before; they were the same ones from Roselle's box truck.

The figure strutted calmly up to the boys, then reached into the kangaroo pouch of their black hoodie —

"Please, we don't have anything!" Vaughn said, fearing the worst.

The figure froze, and cocked their head to the side.

"I beg to differ," the figure said, in a raspy and powerful genderless voice.

The figure's hand emerged from their hoodie pocket with two black business cards. They stepped forward and presented the two cards to Tom and Vaughn, who accepted them without question.

"I believe you have it all."

The figure turned, revealing a large white "X" on the back of their hoodie. As the mercenaries guarded the leader's return to the van, the boys noticed that each of mercenaries also wore the "X" on their uniforms. The masked gang jumped back into their van and sped off down the street.

Tom and Vaughn stood there in utter shock.

Tom glanced down at the black business card, which was made of some kind of weighty metal, and spotted a message that was etched into the card in small white letters. Tom read it aloud:

"*You have been chosen. Tell no one. The liberation depends on you.*"

Vaughn inspected his card. He flipped it over and read out an address that appeared on the back:

"*D train. Kingsbridge Rd. Northbound platform. Second Utility Door.*"

Tom and Vaughn shared a look of bewilderment.

"So... what the hell was that?" Tom asked.

Vaughn didn't know the answer. It was unlike anything he'd witnessed on the streets of the Bronx, but there now existed the possibility that there was an entire world, an entire layer of reality unfolding just beneath the surface, out of the awareness of everyone but a select few.

The ground beneath them began to rumble, and the sounds of a passing subway train emanated through the metal grates on the sidewalk. They both instinctually tracked the path of the slowing train up the block, to where they laid eyes upon a subway staircase that led down to the Uptown D train.

The train stopped, the hydraulics hissed, and Vaughn turned to Tom, who was already nodding vehemently, anticipating the question:

"Wanna find out?"

THE END

Dig the read? Then you'll enjoy the next book of the *BRONXLAND* series, *THE BENJIES*:

A group of Bronx teenagers find a bag full of a million dollars, only to discover that the Benjamins inside possess a deadly curse. When the money gets loose and starts spreading around Manhattan, the kids have no choice but to save the people of New York City — by robbing it all back.

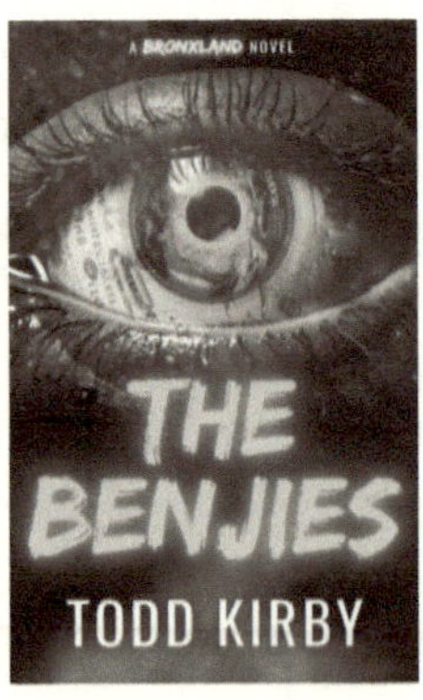

Join the *BRONXLAND* mailing list to receive news about when *THE BENJIES* will be dropping, and other dope updates:

www.welcometobronxland.com